Startled, Hannah gazed at him for a moment.

He'd taken a great deal of trouble to know everything he could about Jonas's twin sons.

"Why?" She asked the question before she had time to think about it. "I mean, why did you take so much trouble?"

He stared down at his shoes for a moment and then met her eyes. "From the time Matthew took me on as an apprentice, I felt as if Jonas was my little brother. It felt good to have someone I could think of as family. Especially after my folks moved out west."

Hannah felt as if she was seeing a different Samuel than she'd ever seen before. Without knowing quite why, she reached out and clasped his hand.

Sam froze for an instant, and then his fingers closed warmly around hers. Hannah's breath quickened.

What was happening to her?

A lifetime spent in rural Pennsylvania and her Pennsylvania Dutch heritage led **Marta Perry** to write about the Plain People who add so much richness to her home state. Marta has seen over seventy of her books published, with over seven million books in print. She and her husband live in a beautiful central Pennsylvania valley noted for its farms and orchards. When she's not writing, she's reading, traveling, baking or enjoying her six beautiful grandchildren.

Books by Marta Perry

Love Inspired

Brides of Lost Creek

Second Chance Amish Bride
The Wedding Quilt Bride
The Promised Amish Bride
The Amish Widow's Heart
A Secret Amish Crush
Nursing Her Amish Neighbor
The Widow's Bachelor Bargain
Match Made at the Amish Inn
The Amish Matchmakers

Visit the Author Profile page at LoveInspired.com for more titles.

THE AMISH MATCHMAKERS

MARTA PERRY

If you purchased this book without a cover you should be aware that this book is stolen property. It was reported as "unsold and destroyed" to the publisher, and neither the author nor the publisher has received any payment for this "stripped book."

ISBN-13: 978-1-335-23019-5

The Amish Matchmakers

Copyright © 2025 by Martha P. Johnson

All rights reserved. No part of this book may be used or reproduced in any manner whatsoever without written permission.

Without limiting the author's and publisher's exclusive rights, any unauthorized use of this publication to train generative artificial intelligence (AI) technologies is expressly prohibited.

This is a work of fiction. Names, characters, places and incidents are either the product of the author's imagination or are used fictitiously. Any resemblance to actual persons, living or dead, businesses, companies, events or locales is entirely coincidental.

For questions and comments about the quality of this book, please contact us at CustomerService@Harlequin.com.

® is a trademark of Harlequin Enterprises ULC.

Love Inspired
22 Adelaide St. West, 41st Floor
Toronto, Ontario M5H 4E3, Canada
www.LoveInspired.com

Printed in U.S.A.

And now abideth faith, hope, charity, these three;
but the greatest of these is charity.
—*1 Corinthians* 13:13

This story is dedicated to my dear husband of sixty-three years, Brian, with all my love.

Chapter One

"Look out!" someone shouted.

Hannah Esch, setting a large platter of cold cuts on the picnic table, looked up in time to see a volleyball coming straight at her. She ducked, reached and grabbed the ball before it could hit the table.

The teenagers grouped on the improvised volleyball court gaped at her, and one of the girls looked ready to cry.

"No problem," Hannah called, and served the ball back onto the court with the skill that had made her one of the first choices for a team when she was a teenager herself. "I might be old, but I can still get the ball."

"Komm play for us, Hannah," one of the boys called out.

She shook her head, smiling. "You want your supper, don't you?"

Dorcas Unger, her friend since their own rumspringa years ago, set down a tray of plates and glasses. "If you're old, I must be as well, so don't be so silly."

"I guess it's wearing black that makes me feel that way." Hannah brushed at the skirt of her black dress. Not every widow in their community held to the tradition of wearing black, but as the bishop's granddaughter, she felt obligated to.

Dorcas shook her head, dismissing the subject. "I thought you were going to come away from that wild volleyball with a black eye," she said. "I should have known better. You always could turn away from troubles with a grin."

Almost before the words were out, Dorcas was shaking her head. "Ach, I'm sorry. I wasn't thinking of Jonas."

"It's all right," Hannah said. Yah, she'd had her share of trouble, losing her young husband to an accident with a chain saw when they'd only been married three years. Still, her five-year-old twins, Will and Elijah, made up for everything else.

As if knowing what she was thinking, Dorcas patted her arm in silent sympathy and then nodded to the game. "It's almost over," she said.

Hannah scanned the serving table. "We'd best get the rest of the food and drink out here. They'll be hungry."

"They're teenagers," Dorcas observed. "They're always hungry." Dorcas's adopted daughter, Katie, was one of the participants, but not her three younger boys. This event was only for the older teenagers of the Lost Creek community. Katie had come to live with Dorcas after her parents died, Katie's uncle Jacob, pursuing his niece, had fallen in love with Dorcas, and they became a family.

The bishop had a few things to say to the teens and their parents. And since the event was being held at their family farm, Hannah felt a responsibility to have things go well.

Not that anything was likely to go wrong with her mother and grandmother in charge of the kitchen. "I'll check to see what else has to come out."

"Good. And I'll make sure no one is snitching anything until we're ready." Dorcas gave a warning look to a couple of boys who had drifted closer to the table. They put on innocent expressions and turned away.

Smiling, Hannah started toward the farmhouse and nearly bumped into the large thermos filled with lemonade that someone was carrying. She grabbed it, helping to set it on the table.

"Sorry," she began, but the word faded on her tongue when she saw who it was: Samuel Miller, the business partner of her late father-in-law. Samuel, who'd done his best to keep Jonas from marrying her. What was he doing here?

Tamping her feelings down at coming face-to-face with him so abruptly, Hannah managed to greet him with a cool nod. Before he could respond, she darted off toward the farmhouse.

The large farmhouse that had sheltered the Stoltz family for generations sprawled out, with two entrances on this side—one into the grossdaadi haus, where her grandfather and grandmother lived, and the other into the kitchen of the main house. That was her destination right now.

Focus on the work to be done, she ordered herself, not on what Sam Miller was doing here.

The screen door banged behind her as she rushed into the kitchen. She wasn't alone. Mammi was lifting pans of pizza from the oven and setting them on the long wooden table. Hannah's grandmother was mixing a large bowl of potato salad, and her grandfather, Bishop Thomas, was reaching over her shoulder to snitch a spoonful.

"Stop that." Grossmammi shook her wooden spoon at him. "I'll give you a swat with this spoon if I see you reaching in again."

"Ach, you wouldn't treat your sweetheart that way, would you?" Winking at Hannah, he bent over to plant a kiss on his wife's cheek.

Grossmammi gestured as if she'd swat him, but she glanced at Hannah instead. "What am I going to do with a bishop who behaves that way?"

Teasing back and forth was usual between her and her grandparents, but Hannah's thoughts were too involved with the appearance of Samuel in their backyard to tease back.

Instead, she frowned at her grandfather. "Why didn't you tell me Samuel Miller was going to be here? He's surely not going to be one of the chaperones, is he?"

Her grandfather's lean, weathered face could look firm and dignified when he was preaching, but when he studied her, his expression always held the love he felt for each of his many children and grandchildren. She'd never felt lost in the crowd with Grossdaadi.

Several girls clattered in carrying empty trays, and after a glance, Grossdaadi held out his hand to her. "Komm," he said gently. Hannah took his hand, and he propelled her into the pantry, out of range of the chattering girls.

Her resentment was fading in the face of his love, but Hannah tried to hold on to it. "You could have told me about him."

"I could," he agreed. "But you tell me. Have you forgiven Samuel yet for influencing Jonas against your marriage?"

Hannah opened her lips and then closed them again. How could she claim she'd forgiven Samuel when just the sight of him sent anger surging through her?

"No?" he asked after a moment's silence.

She tried not to meet his eyes, and she sought to justify herself. "Sam's opinion meant a lot to Jonas. His attitude hurt him." Her throat tightened. "Samuel was like an older brother to him. To have Samuel turn against our marriage broke his heart."

She said it defensively, but even as she did, she knew that the church wouldn't accept that as an excuse. *Forgive as you would be forgiven.* That was the Amish way. The hard path.

"You haven't got there yet, ain't so? So maybe working together on this project with the teens will give you the opportunity to leave that feeling in the past, ain't so?"

Hannah took a deep breath. He wasn't speaking just as her much-loved grandfather but also as her bishop. She didn't really have any choice as to her answer.

Staring down at the wide oak boards of the floor, she looked for a way out but didn't find one. Finally, Hannah managed to speak. "I... I'll try."

She would, she promised herself. But even while her grandfather was hugging her, an unworthy thought sneaked into her mind. Samuel wasn't related to the bishop. And Samuel couldn't be any happier about this than she was. Maybe *he* would back out.

She stepped away, hoping she wasn't betraying her thoughts. Whether Samuel did or didn't, she had no choice but to go ahead with this project.

The meal was down to dessert and coffee when Hannah, sitting at a picnic table with Dorcas and Dorcas's husband, Jacob, saw her grandfather rise slowly to his feet. The chattering died away and all eyes turned to him.

Everyone here knew what he had to say, of course. Word spread quickly in the Amish community. When the bishop and the ministers of their worshipping group and the one most closely associated with them started talking about the high rate of inherited conditions among babies in their two congregations, everyone knew about it and shared their concern.

Hannah couldn't help a glance at Dorcas. Dorcas's younger sister, Sarry, had been a Down syndrome child. She knew Dorcas's feelings... Sarry was a precious, deeply loved and loving person, and they wouldn't trade her for anyone. But there were other inherited conditions, some bringing much more serious and painful results.

That was why Dorcas and Jacob were part of the group of chaperones. They wanted to show their support in the most practical way.

"...we love every child as a precious gift of God," Bishop Thomas was saying quietly. "By helping our young adults get to know others their age from different communities, we hope they may grow to love someone who has a different inheritance, resulting in healthier babies. Surely this is pleasing to our Lord."

Dorcas leaned over to whisper in Hannah's ear. "He's doing it well. Your grandfather is a wise man."

Hannah nodded in agreement. Grossdaadi was wise, and it was the right thing they were doing. Not everyone would agree, of course.

A small voice whispered in the back of her mind. *Maybe your grandfather is right about you, as well. Forgiving Samuel honestly and completely might free you from some of the guilt you feel.*

She let her gaze drift to the next table, where Samuel sat at the end of a bench. At rest, concentrating on the bishop, his face showed none of the seriousness that Jonas had always said hid a warm heart.

Samuel glanced toward her suddenly, their gazes meeting, and she felt as if she'd been doused in a bucket of hot water. Had he seen that? He could hardly help it, could he?

Focusing on her grandfather again, she found him talking about their first visit from a community over in western Pennsylvania. They'd be here for a weekend of service projects and fun times together. She felt a moment of panic at the thought of spending that much time in Samuel's company.

If forgiveness was the only thing that could cure this, she'd best find it quickly.

As the event drew to a close, Samuel watched the flames of the bonfire die down. The logs at the base glowed, providing perfect heat for the marshmallows some of the youngsters were toasting on long sticks. The circle of light surrounding the bonfire lit up the young faces, giving them a rosy glow.

Once he'd have been one of them, stuffing himself with just one more marshmallow. Usually there'd be someone who wanted to try to beat everyone else with the number of marshmallows consumed, even if he ended up rolling on the ground clutching his belly.

Those days seemed a very long time ago now...back when he had a sweetheart of his own, when Sam had been a young apprentice with Jonas's father, willingly keeping an eye on the boy who had no siblings.

A golden-brown marshmallow on the end of a stick appeared in front of him, scattering the memories. He glanced behind the stick to find Hannah, her black dress blending into the surrounding darkness.

"Take it," she urged, wobbling the marshmallow in front of his face. "One of the boys did it for me, but if I eat it, I won't be responsible for the consequences."

He relaxed at the comfortable note in Hannah's voice. Maybe she'd decided it was time to give up her grudge against him. If they'd ever been in competition over Jonas, then she had won, hadn't she?

Samuel took the marshmallow delicately and slid it off the stick, careful to get both the crisp outer shell and the hot, sticky interior, thinking it must be a peace offering.

"Denke. You'll let me be sick instead, yah?"

"You're too tough for that, surely." She sat down, leaning against the back of the bench her brothers had pulled out for the occasion.

He popped the marshmallow into his mouth. "Perfect," he managed to articulate. "So, what do you think? Are we going to be able to manage this crew?"

Hannah looked around the circle of faces. "If we can't, it's going to be a long summer. But I think they'll be all right. I hope," she added.

Sam couldn't hold back a chuckle. "I don't know why Bishop Thomas wants me involved. I'd have expected the chaperones to be married couples."

"Don't look at me for an answer," Hannah

seemed to make an effort to keep her voice light. "My grandfather didn't confide in me. And it's hard to say no to him."

"You're right about that." He certain sure hadn't been able to, but then, he hadn't known it would put him into close contact with Hannah.

Still, it was a good thing, he reminded himself. He needed to talk with Hannah about the harness business and her father-in-law's wishes. She didn't know everything she should.

Matthew Esch had trusted Samuel to take care of his share of the business for Hannah and her twins. That was reasonable since no one in Hannah's family had knowledge or interest in the business.

Simple, but it had been difficult to explain anything when Hannah put up barriers whenever he came near her.

Still, this encounter with Hannah was going better than he'd expected. Maybe she was ready to let go of the past, or at least, his part of it. Losing Jonas wouldn't be something she'd ever forget.

Even as he tried to come up with a way to keep the conversation going, he realized she had turned to look behind them at the farmhouse. He followed her gaze. Two small faces showed at a second-floor window. Apparently, the twins were up.

Hannah waved, then the boys waved, and in a moment the boys had vanished from the window. A few minutes later, the twins were running barefoot across the damp grass toward Hannah. They skirted around him and squeezed into Hannah's welcoming arms.

"Now what are you doing still awake?" Her voice was half scolding, half laughing.

"We couldn't go to sleep." The twins were identical, but Sam guessed that was probably Will, the outgoing one. Elijah was content to give a vigorous nod.

"You mean you weren't trying," Hannah said.

If she was trying to sound firm, Samuel suspected it wasn't working. He had to smile. Jonas's sons were about the age their father had been when Samuel had come to Lost Creek as an apprentice.

Will sent a cautious look at him and then smiled, apparently reassured. The boys looked a lot like Hannah right now, their cheeks rosy from the firelight and blue eyes sparkling.

"We tried to go to sleep," Will said plaintively. "Honest, Mammi."

"We wanted to see the fire." Elijah's voice was surprising—soft and gruff instead of clear and light like his twin's.

Hannah snuggled them close, bending to kiss

the tops of their heads. "Just a few minutes," she murmured. "Then you have to go up."

Love shone in her face and sounded in her voice, and Samuel's heart winced.

He still had promises to keep—promises to Matthew and even to Jonas. They were both gone now, and the sooner he talked to Hannah, the better.

No. He corrected that. Not just talked. Persuaded. He had to convince her to let him do what he'd promised.

Sam glanced down at Will. His eyes were closed, and he lay against Hannah like a cloth doll, falling asleep that quickly. Elijah, his lashes drooping, looked a minute behind him.

Sam's lips twitched as he met Hannah's gaze, the two sleepy children between them. She was smiling, and for a moment it was as if the chasm between them had never existed.

This moment gave him the opportunity to say what he needed to, if only he could find the right words.

"If Jonas were here…" he began.

The moment shattered like glass breaking. Hannah's eyes went from smiling to furious in an instant.

"Don't." She slung the word at him as if it were a stone. "Don't pretend to know what Jonas would do if he were here. I don't want to hear anything you have to say about him."

Scooping Will up in her arms and clasping Elijah's hand, she rose to her feet.

Samuel jumped up, reaching out to help her, but she evaded his grasp. Her expression suggested that if he touched her, she'd shout at him. Of course she wouldn't. Hannah had too much control for that. But she'd put up a barrier between them he couldn't possibly break through, at least not now.

Will moved in his mother's arms, snuggling his face into the curve of Hannah's neck and sighing. Hannah murmured something soothing, turned and walked away toward the house with the twins. It looked as if Hannah not only wouldn't be willing to work with him, she undoubtedly wouldn't want him on the chaperone list at all.

Chapter Two

Hearing the thump of little feet in the hallway the next morning, Hannah pushed in a final pin to secure her kapp over her hair. Now the footsteps were on the stairs down to the kitchen, and she hurried out into the hallway to see the twins disappearing downstairs to breakfast.

Usually she woke up before them, but last night she'd stayed awake late, going over and over her encounter with Sam. Her anger had faded, at least a little. She could hardly forbid Sam to mention her husband's name, much as she would like to. Grossdaadi had been right—she had to find a way to deal with Samuel, if for no other reason than the fact that after Jonas's death, his father had left his share of leather shop to the twins in trust. And that trust was controlled by Samuel Miller until the boys were twenty-one, so she didn't have an option.

As she entered the kitchen, Mammi was shoveling scrambled eggs onto the boys' plates. She glanced at Hannah and then looked again. Obviously, Hannah was doing a terrible job of hiding her feelings.

Planting a smile on her face, Hannah shook her head slightly at her mother. They had to talk, but only when Will and Elijah were safely out of earshot. Reaching over Will's head, she steadied his hand as he dipped a spoonful of black raspberry jam from the jar onto his toast.

"Denke, Mammi." He smiled at her. "I don't want to lose any."

"I want some, too," Elijah announced predictably, grabbing at the jar before Will could take any more.

Before Will could set up a howl, their grandmother spoke. "There is plenty of blackcap jam," she said, using the local term for the black raspberries. "Don't you remember when your mammi and I had that big kettle filled with jam last fall?"

"The whole house smelled like jam," Elijah said, eyes wide.

"We loved it," Will added. "Will you do it again this year?"

"If you boys will pick us enough berries, we will," Hannah's mother reassured them.

Hannah watched her mother dealing with her grandchildren in the same way she had coped with her own large family—lovingly and firmly, always holding out a picture of the good results that came from working hard.

Mammi was the rock of the family. That was one reason why it was so important to have her on Hannah's side in this matter of dealing with Samuel.

When the boys had carried their plates to the sink, they went at their usual run out the back door to find their grandfather. Whatever he was doing, they'd want to help him, and he'd always find something useful they could do.

For a moment, Hannah stood staring after them until Mammi handed her a dish towel. "Worrying?" she asked.

"No, not at all," Hannah said quickly. "Just thinking."

Mammi's blue eyes rested on her, as if seeing more than Hannah said. "You had words with Sam again last night, ain't so?"

Hannah felt the warmth come up in her cheeks, and she tried not to meet her mother's gaze. "I didn't mean to, but I wish Jonas's father hadn't tied up the business the way he did."

"Samuel is a craftsman, and a good businessman, too," her mother commented. "You can surely count on him to keep it in fine shape for the boys."

Mammi seemed to expect an answer, so Hannah nodded. "I suppose so, but—"

"But you haven't forgiven him for being against you and Jonas marrying."

There it was again. Even her mother sounded like the bishop. It was as if they were plotting together to push her into getting along with Samuel. She seemed to hear Jonas's voice in her thoughts.

They don't understand. Not even Samuel, and I thought sure he would. I always thought he was on my side.

Hannah had seen the pain in his eyes at that betrayal. Samuel had been like an idolized older brother to Jonas, and Samuel had let him down.

Her mother put a wet plate into Hannah's hand, and Hannah started drying in circular movements.

"I'm sure Sam was trying to be faithful to what Jonas's father wanted," Mammi said, "and Matthew thought you were too young for marriage."

"We were both eighteen." Hannah could hear the defensiveness in her voice. "After all, you and Daadi were married at that age. And you didn't forbid us to marry." She wondered, as she often did, why they hadn't.

Mammi was silent for a moment. "We thought Matthew was wrong in the way he handled his son, and we didn't want to push you into a situation where you'd run away. Were we wrong?"

Hannah shook her head silently. Would that have pushed her and Jonas into something even worse? Or would it have turned out the same way, no matter what anyone said?

"Maybe we weren't very mature." At least, Jonas hadn't been. "But I wouldn't trade Will and Elijah for anything in the world."

Her mother clasped her hand for a moment. "Yah. Sometimes in raising kinder all you can do is put them in God's hands and let it work out according to His will. That's what we did."

Comforted, Hannah nodded, but she couldn't help thinking that it didn't answer the question in her mind. Wasn't it possible to forgive Samuel without seeing too much of him?

Sam pulled up to the hitching rail by the Stoltz barn on Monday afternoon, noticing that nothing was left of yesterday's activities except a few ashes in the burn circle. He wasn't surprised. Simon Stoltz, Hannah's father, was a great one for cleaning up as you go, and his wife was the same way. He would no sooner leave the picnic remnants to clean up today than his wife would leave dirty dishes in the sink.

Swinging himself down from the buggy, Sam pulled out the bag containing the tools of his trade that always traveled with him. Simon had wanted a new harness for the Shetland pony that pulled the pony cart before his grandsons started driving it.

He glanced toward the farmhouse, but Hannah wasn't in sight. Still, no matter how she resisted it, they had to have a talk about the future of the harness shop.

Simon came hurrying from the shed and pulled open the barn door. "Right on time, I see. I kept the pony in the stall this morning, otherwise that clever mare would pick today not to be caught. She's gotten spoiled with not being driven much lately."

Sam nodded, coming inside and putting his tools down before removing his jacket and hanging it over the end of an empty stall. "Ponies tend to be like that…as if they were born with an extra dose of mischief."

"Ginger sure enough is." He led the pale golden pony out of her stall and fastened her in the crossties. She was so fluffy that she looked like a stuffed toy. "I've been thinking—"

But it seemed Sam wouldn't hear what his thoughts were, because the twins rushed into the barn, clearly excited.

"Are you here to start the new harness?" Will tugged at Sam's hand, while Elijah paused to pet the mare, who nuzzled him in return. "Can we watch?"

"If your grossdaadi says it's all right." Sam

nodded toward Simon, who smiled indulgently at the two boys with their identical pale blue shirts, dark blue suspenders and summer straw hats.

"Just don't get in Samuel's way," Simon cautioned. "He has lots of work on hand besides Ginger's harness."

"The new harness is because we're going to learn to drive," Will piped up. "We'll both be good at that." He darted a look at his brother. "I might be better because I'm older."

"Only ten minutes, Mammi says," Elijah pointed out.

"And don't go bragging about what you can do when you haven't even tried it," his grandfather added.

Will shrugged, then came to peer into Samuel's tool bag. "I think I can," he muttered, not loud enough for his grandfather to hear. Samuel did, and he had to suppress a smile. Keeping ahead of these two boys must be quite a job.

Sam pulled out the cloth tape measure, nearly hitting Will's head with it as the boy leaned over, eyes curious.

"That's like Mammi's sewing measure," he announced. "Grossdaadi has a big long metal one that snaps back if you push a button. You could use it."

"Yah, I have one like that, too, but this one is special to use for measuring your pony's face."

Elijah hurried over to hold the pony's halter as he approached. "Ginger wouldn't like metal on her face, I don't think." Again, the gruff little voice surprised him.

"That's right. A lot of horses are fussy about anything that goes on their heads. I had one once that wouldn't let anyone touch her ears. She'd rear and kick if I tried it."

"Why?" Both boys asked him at the same time. Curiosity seemed to be a common trait with Hannah's children.

He shrugged, not wanting to suggest that someone might have hurt the mare's ears. "Lots of horses, and people, are." He reached out to tug Elijah's ear lightly.

"It didn't hurt a bit," Elijah announced, reaching out as if to do the same to his brother.

Samuel intercepted him just in time. "Let's not keep trying it." He'd best be careful of what he said to these boys. Making friends with them was his aim for the day, not giving Hannah another reason to be annoyed with him.

He'd been fourteen when he'd come into the harness trade as Matthew's apprentice, and a few years later, when the rest of his family moved out to Indiana, he'd stayed here in Lost Creek. It always felt like home to him, and he'd gone from being Matthew's apprentice to being his partner.

Now he was running the business on his own, and these two boys were the future.

The twins were pushing close to him, one on either side. "Who wants to help me measure for the harness?" he asked.

"Me, me," Will said, jumping up and down eagerly, and Elijah nodded, his hat bobbing. It said a lot for the pony's disposition that she just regarded the boys mildly.

Hannah's father answered the question he hadn't even asked. "Ginger knows youngsters after all the boys and girls she's taught to drive. Worst thing she'll do is stop dead and look at them."

"Good to know. Some ponies can be temperamental." He put his hand on Will's shoulder, calming him. "It's still just as well not to act excited around animals. Any animals."

"That's what Grossdaadi says." Elijah stroked the thick, fluffy winter growth that lingered on the pony's neck.

"He knows, yah?" He passed the cloth measure over to Elijah. "Now you start measuring around her muzzle just here."

"What about me?" Will didn't want to be left out.

"Now you catch the tape when your bruder passes it over to this side and bring it across." He guided the boy's small hand. "Good job." He took a second look at the number, checking how tight the tape was.

For the next few minutes, the three of them worked together, measuring and writing down the figures that would help him make a headstall that was a perfect fit, he trusted. It was important that this one be just right.

Samuel felt a flow of satisfaction. This was how Matthew had taught him—showing him how to do each step, standing beside him and letting him try. There was pleasure in doing the same thing with Matthew's grandsons.

It had been the sorrow of Matthew's life that his own son had no interest in the business. If Jonas had been a little more mature, if Matthew had been a little more patient... Well, if Samuel could draw Matthew's grandsons into the pleasure of crafting something so satisfying and useful, it might go a long way toward repaying Matthew's kindness to him.

"What will you do next?" Will asked, handing him the tape as he began packing up.

"Next, I'll be working in our shop, because I'll need the big sewing machine to stitch the leather pieces together. I can't do that part by hand."

Elijah was leaning against the pony's strong shoulder, and in return Ginger rested her head on his. "I'd like to try that."

Here was an opening to what he wanted, and

he was almost afraid to take it. He glanced at Simon and seemed to read approval in his expression.

"Maybe you can, if your mammi lets you come to the shop one day soon."

"We'll ask her." Will spun toward the door with one of his quick movements.

Samuel followed his movement. Hannah stood just inside the door, watching them. How long had she been standing there?

Hannah paused, watching her sons lean on Samuel, their faces alive with interest. For an instant the image froze, and she imagined Jonas standing there. Then the pony nudged Elijah with her head, and the picture broke up with laughter.

Will came running to her, with his twin close behind. "Can we, Mammi? Can we go see how Samuel makes the new harness for Ginger?"

"Slow down," she said, putting her hand on Will's shoulder so that he'd stop jumping up and down. She'd heard Daad say something about ordering a new harness for the pony but hadn't realized Samuel was coming today.

Samuel met her gaze with a rueful expression. "Sorry. I did say they'd have to ask you."

"And they jumped on ahead of you, yah? I know how that goes." She knew, none better, how the boys went flying off, jumping to conclusions.

Still, couldn't Samuel have waited for her before getting the boys excited about going to the shop?

"The boys were helping to measure Ginger for the harness," Daad said, unhooking the pony from the crossties. "Komm, the two of you. You can help me put Ginger in the paddock."

"But Mammi…" Will began, but Elijah tugged at his shirt.

"You heard Grossdaadi. You want to open the gate or lead Ginger in?"

It amused her to hear Elijah distracting his brother's attention just as her daad would do. Elijah might be ten minutes younger, but in some ways he was more mature, she thought, than Will. They went off peacefully with their grossdaadi, leaving her with Samuel. He was staring after the boys.

"Are you thinking that they are like Jonas?" The question she asked wasn't at all what she'd had in mind to say.

Samuel turned to her, shaking his head. "I was thinking how different they are, in spite of looking exactly alike." His lips twitched slightly, as if laughing at himself.

She was so pleased at his perception that she forgot to scold him. "They are identical. Jonas used to tease me by saying maybe I'd mixed them up."

Now she'd mentioned Jonas to him, something she'd been determined not to do. With more tact than she'd have expected from him, Samuel didn't follow it up by saying something about Jonas.

"I don't know about when they were babies, but now you can tell as soon as they speak, ain't so?"

She nodded, smiling, and then tried to remember that she was annoyed with him.

"I'd rather you didn't talk to them about the business. At least, not unless I'm here."

"I didn't," he said shortly, and then took a deep breath. "Sorry. Let's start again. They asked what I would do next on the harness, and I told them. If you were listening, you heard me say they'd have to ask you."

"Yah." She looked anywhere except at his face. "You're right. I just… I don't see why Jonas's father left everything the way he did."

Even without looking, Hannah felt him take a step closer to her.

"That's what I wanted to talk to you about. Will you give me a few minutes?"

One part of her wanted to scurry away, but that would be childish, and she knew it. Instead, she sat down on a convenient bale of straw and folded her hands in her lap. "I'm listening."

Sam sat down next to her on the prickly seat.

She stole a glance at him, and she realized he didn't know how to begin.

After a moment of indecision, he seemed to force himself. "Matthew was my partner for a long time. Naturally he talked to me about what he'd do with his half of the business." He swallowed, and she saw his Adam's apple move. "I think he told Jonas that he'd leave it to him, but in trust until he was twenty-one."

She nodded, remembering clearly how furious and hurt Jonas had been when he'd found out. "Leaving you in charge."

Hannah thought she'd kept her voice level, but he must have read something into it.

"He wanted to be sure that no quick decision could put my share in jeopardy. Whether he was right or not, I don't know."

"It didn't come up," she said, her throat going tight at the memory of a neighbor rushing in to tell them about Jonas's accident.

"No." His voice sounded as if his throat was equally tight. "I felt that Matthew didn't know what to do for the best. In his grief, he seemed to lose all interest."

"Including in his grandsons," she snapped, the memory rankling.

Samuel's sleeve brushed hers as he shrugged. "I can't explain it. I can just promise you that I'll do my best to keep the business in good shape for the twins."

"Do you resent the fact that it's half theirs?" The question came out before she could stop it.

He looked at her, his eyes widening. "No, of course not. That's only what's right, and what's owing to both Jonas and Matthew. I do think it would be better if you'd let them get used to the business while they're young."

Hannah couldn't doubt his sincerity. Her grandfather's words about forgiveness flowed through her mind. At least, she had to give it a chance.

She stood up, brushing her skirt off. "We'd best go in before the boys try to bring a snack out to us." They moved together and stepped out into the sunlight that fell on their faces. Blinking, Hannah glanced up at him.

"All right," she said, though there was doubt in her eyes. "When do you want me to bring the boys in? Tomorrow?"

It wasn't a full agreement to his plans. She wasn't ready to do that just now. But it was a start.

Chapter Three

Hannah stepped out onto the back porch the next morning. Today she had committed to take the twins into the harness shop, and she felt a little queasy about it. She thought she was doing the right thing, but how could she be sure?

Both her mother and her grandmother were sitting there on the porch. Her mother was making a pretense of being totally involved with the rhubarb she was cleaning, but Grossmammi watched her with a question in her faded blue eyes.

"You're off to the shop, ain't so?" she asked.

"Not quite yet. The boys were so excited about going that I thought they'd never settle down, so I reminded them that their chores came first."

"You could have let them skip their chores today," Mammi suggested, but there was laughter in her eyes.

"I was tempted to let them off, but I remembered that you and Daadi didn't raise us that way. You always told us kids we had to finish our chores before we ran off to do anything else. You're not changing your mind, are you?"

Her mother's face crinkled with laughter. "Grandchildren are different. But don't worry. I won't interfere."

"I know. You're good about that, not like Jonas's mother."

She had a flash of memory. Jonas's mother had been so pleased at having a baby that nothing would do but that he should have everything he wanted. That wasn't a good thing for any child.

Grossmammi seemed to follow her thoughts without difficulty. "Poor woman. She had lost so many babies that it was no wonder she spoiled him."

In the end, it wasn't good for Jonas, growing up to think everything should come easily to him. Disappointment was all the sharper when it inevitably came…disappointment and an urge to try everything, no matter how dangerous.

Hannah tried to push that particular memory out of her mind, knowing it would lead, as always, to the day when he borrowed a chain saw, thinking he didn't need any help to prune the pines he was growing for sale.

She would never, *ever* say anything about that to the twins. They would grow up believing that their father had been as wise and powerful as they'd thought him when they were almost three.

Her mother got up, carrying the bowl of rhubarb. "I made lunches for the three of you, so don't forget them when you're ready to go." She disappeared into the kitchen, letting the screen door clatter behind her.

Hannah looked after her, then at her grandmother. What was in Mammi's mind about involving the twins in a visit to the harness shop? Did she think Hannah was wrong to agree? Or was she leaving them alone so that Grossmammi could give her good advice?

"It's the right thing to do," her grandmother said, once again reading her expression easily. "You must let the boys get acquainted with the business that would have belonged to their father if things had been different. Your mother knows that. She's just trying to protect you, as well as them."

"She doesn't need to protect me," Hannah protested. "Sam doesn't know very much about little boys, though. I don't want him to let them try anything they're not ready for."

"You'll be there," Grossmammi reminded her. Her forehead crinkled, the fine lines webbing out from her eyes. "That's as it should be, Hannah. You know that, don't you?"

Hannah avoided her eyes. Unlike Grossdaadi, her grandmother tended to come out bluntly with what needed to be said. Hannah braced herself.

"It's been four months since Matthew Esch passed. It's time you got used to the way things are."

"I just think—"

Grossmammi was already shaking her head. "Matthew Esch wanted to do the best for his grandsons. He trusted Samuel to see to it. Now it's time you trusted Samuel, too. At least where the business is concerned."

Her grandmother reached out, and Hannah took her hand, feeling the fine, fragile bones and wondering that there was still so much strength in the warm clasp.

Her grandmother was right, of course. Hannah couldn't deprive her boys of the business that would rightfully be theirs, and that meant she had to find a way to work with Samuel.

"I'll try." She didn't sound convinced, and she realized that her grandmother must know it.

But Grossmammi seemed satisfied, patting Hannah's hand before releasing it. "And here they come."

Hannah looked up. Daad drove the small buggy toward them, the boys seated one on each side of him.

"Look at us, Mammi. Grossdaadi let us hitch up Ginger," Will called. "He said we did a gut job."

"Except for forgetting the lines on one side," Elijah added. "We'll remember next time."

"I'm glad to hear it." She glanced at her father to find him smiling, so they must have done all right.

"Can we go now?" Will bounced on his seat. "We're all ready."

"Not until you wash your face and hands and use the bathroom," she said. Will never wanted to wait for anything, so some things still needed a reminder.

With a little grumbling on Will's part, the twins slid down and ran inside, nearly running into their grandmother on the way.

"Sorry," Hannah said, swinging herself up to the buggy seat. Her mother just shook her head.

"Here are the lunches." She handed up three paper bags, which Hannah stowed under the seat. "And don't think you have to be back at any certain time. Stay as long as you want."

Apparently, her whole family thought this was a good thing. Today's experience would tell her whether she could agree with them.

Samuel glanced toward the clock on the back wall of the harness shop. The hands seemed to be moving more slowly than usual.

"You want me to bring the clock up here?" Joseph Shuler, his part-time leather worker for more years than he could remember, chuckled, his sparse gray beard waggling.

"You couldn't reach it, ain't so?" Sam retorted, teasing him back.

Joseph nudged him in the ribs. "You're getting eager to see Hannah, yah?"

If he was, Sam certain sure wasn't going to admit it to Joseph. The old man was just as good at gossip as any two women, and he didn't want any foolish chatter to reach Hannah's ears.

"Ach, you know better than that. I want this to go well for Matthew's grandsons, that's all."

Joseph sobered. "They'll need to be more interested in the business than their daadi ever was."

He could only nod. Both knew that Matthew's wife hadn't wanted her only son to spend his life in the harness shop.

Samuel had never understood why. It was a good business, always bringing in enough for them to live comfortably. What else could she have wanted for Jonas?

With a glance out the window at the hitching rail along the side of the building, Samuel returned to sorting the ready-made halters that hung on the side rack. The front of the shop was given over to items that the Englisch customers might need. Horse people from as far as two counties away came to shop here, and when they did, they'd pick up all kinds of horse-related items. He had to carry what they wanted, or they'd go elsewhere.

In the rear of the building was where the real work of the business went on. Three heavy-duty leather sewing machines were connected by a belt that ran down through the floor to power them. Joseph was already sitting at his favorite machine, absorbed in the tool belt he was making.

The bell on the front door jingled, and he turned to see two Englisch couples come in, hung about with cameras and obviously tourists. Despite the sign of the door saying No Photos, one of the men was already lifting his camera, aiming it toward Samuel.

Before he could speak, another Englisch customer came in behind them. Aileen Chapel, a local horsewoman, reached out to block the camera. When the man, red-faced, turned to her, she gave him a smile.

"No pictures, please. We want to respect the owner's beliefs, don't we?"

The firm voice and the charming smile worked wonders. Not only did the man's momentary annoyance seep away, but he also smiled and babbled something about not knowing.

Aileen had defused the situation, and unless he didn't understand his customers, the tourists would find something, however unlikely, to buy. They'd want to prove they weren't prejudiced against the Amish.

Sam moved behind the counter as Aileen approached it. "Denke," he murmured.

"Funny, how people can stare right at the sign and then think it doesn't apply to them." She turned the smile on him.

It was not part of his business to flirt with the customers, but Aileen was a good customer, and he'd have to chat with her a bit. She launched into a tale of the troubles she'd had with a horse she was boarding for someone. He smiled and nodded and tried to respond, all the while taking quick glances at the door. He wanted to see Hannah and the twins coming, but he'd appreciate it if they'd wait until he got some of these people out of the shop.

Today was important. It would be the first time in over a year that Hannah had brought the children in. If everything went well, if the boys were interested, even enthusiastic, he could probably convince Hannah to make it a regular thing.

Joseph could take over the cash box if necessary, but Joseph didn't care to wait on the Englisch customers. For someone who talked so much, he was inarticulate in Englisch.

Aileen ended her talk about how ignorant her client was with a laugh and a light touch on his arm. He was just responding when the bell jingled and Hannah and the twins entered.

The boys spotted him right away and rushed toward him, their straw hats bobbing. Hannah stopped where she was, looking from him to Aileen with an expression he couldn't quite read. Disapproving, maybe? Something that darkened her blue eyes, anyway.

Then the twins were there, both chattering away with excitement. "We came," Will announced. "Mammi said we would."

"After we did our chores," Elijah added.

"Well, now," Aileen said, face crinkling with laughter as she looked from one to the other. "Who are these fine youngsters? I didn't know you had a family."

"I don't." He hushed the boys, switching to Pennsylvania Dutch. "Calm down, now. We have customers in the shop. This is Ms. Chapel. She boards riding horses for people."

They looked at Aileen, blue eyes widening identically, and for just a second he found himself wishing they really were his.

"Their grandfather was my partner in the shop. I hope they'll be partners here, too, one day," he said to Aileen.

Hannah came up behind the boys and put a hand on each of them, as if to remind him that the decision was up to her. And right now, she didn't look favorably impressed.

Hannah was taken aback by seeing Samuel chatting and at ease with the woman at the counter. She'd seldom seen him so relaxed and outgoing. It was a big difference from the way he generally looked at her.

The voice of her conscience whispered in her ear, sounding very much like her grandmother, asked what she'd said or done to give Samuel a reason to relax with her.

The woman was flirting with Samuel, she told herself. It might have been a few years ago for her, but a woman didn't forget the signs. She recognized the way the woman tilted her head, glancing up under her lashes with a small, private smile. She even put her hand on Sam's arm when he handed her change.

The boys were getting restless. She could feel them fidgeting under her hands. In a moment Will would burst into the conversation.

"Samuel is busy with a customer. Let's go back and see what Joseph is doing." She guided them firmly around the counter. As soon as they spotted the big sewing machines, they spurted away toward Joseph.

The old man looked up at them with a big grin. "Here are the twins. Let's see if I can tell." He studied them carefully through the thick glasses he wore. Then he reached out and touched Will's chest. "You're Elijah, ain't so?"

Will shook his head, both the twins giggling, always pleased when folks mixed them up. "I'm Will," he said, standing tall. "This is Elijah." He poked his brother's chest.

Joseph did a double take. "Are you sure?"

They giggled again. "Sure, we're sure," Will said. "We always know who we are."

"Ach, I guess you would." He spread out the belt he'd been stitching. "What do you think of this?"

Elijah reached out, looking at Joseph to be sure it was all right. At Joseph's nod, he stroked the belt. "Soft," he said.

"Leather is strong, but you want it to be soft as well, so it won't feel like it's poking into you. Maybe one day you'll need a tool belt like this, yah?"

They nodded. "Grossdaadi has one like that," Elijah said.

The bell jangled again as the customers made their way out, including the flirtatious woman, waving back over her shoulder. But Samuel had already turned toward Hannah. In a moment he stood next to her.

"Sorry about that, but customers are important. You know why?" He looked from Will to Elijah.

"They give you money for what you made." Elijah spoke first, surprising her.

"Right. Sometimes we might make something for a present, though. Like that tool belt Joseph is making for his son's birthday."

"When I get bigger, I want a tool belt," Will announced.

Joseph gestured them closer so they could see how he stitched it. Sam used the opportunity to move nearer to her. "Sorry I was tied up with customers when you came."

"We understand." She pictured the woman touching Sam's arm and then chased the image away. She couldn't possibly say anything about it... Goodness, Sam might think she was jealous.

Horrified at the thought, she backed away from it. Of course she wasn't jealous. She didn't have those kinds of feelings for Samuel. She never would.

Hannah watched as he showed the boys the different parts of the sewing machine. She could see from here that Elijah was fascinated by the way it worked. Will, in contrast, wanted to climb on the seat and make it go.

Sam lifted him on the seat and held him steady while he tried to reach the treadle with his feet. "When your legs get a little longer, you'll do it."

Will slid down, wrinkling his nose. "Everything we want to do is wait till you're older. I don't want to wait."

Sam ruffled his hair, smiling, and then put the straw hat back on it. "We all feel like that, don't we, Hannah?"

"Seems that way," she agreed. She caught a glimpse of Elijah, trying to fit his hand through the slot that took the cable down through the floor. "'Lijah, don't do that. You might get stuck."

"Joseph's keeping an eye out for them," Sam said quietly. "He won't start until everything is clear."

Elijah, looking a little red, stood up.

"We'll go down to the cellar in a little bit and you can see how it works, okay?" Samuel said, and Elijah's face cleared as he nodded.

She had to admit that for a man who didn't have children of his own, Samuel showed a lot of understanding.

"Do you think Mammi should try it?" he asked.

Naturally, the boys clamored immediately for her to take the seat, and before she could think of an excuse, Sam was helping her onto it.

"Just put your hands here to guide the leather." He moved them to the right place on a piece of scrap leather. "And then use the treadle like you would a regular sewing machine."

He reached across and touched the treadle, and

the leather jerked forward, startling her. "See, just like sewing a new dress." His face was close enough that she felt his breath against her cheek.

"Not quite the same," she said quickly. "Can I get down now?"

"For sure." Taking her hand, he helped her get clear of the machine. They stood close together for a moment, and Joseph called the twins over to show them something.

"That didn't scare you off, did it?" he asked, and she took a careful step away, freeing her hand.

"No, of course not. Don't be silly. It's like our sewing machine, only bigger."

"I was thinking about the situation." Samuel hesitated for a moment, looking down at the worn floorboards, scarred where the machines stood. "It seems like you have an interest in the business until the boys are grown, just like I do. Maybe it would be a good idea if you and the boys were to come in an afternoon or two a week."

She opened her mouth to protest, but he held up his hand to stop her.

"Hear me out. We're at the point where we need some extra help to handle the customers, so I don't have to keep leaving work to wait on them. If you could do that, it'd be good for the business, and you could bring the boys in as often as you like." He gave her a long look. "Think about it, anyway."

She'd come in here ready to find an excuse for backing out. Seeing Samuel when they were with the teenagers and then in the shop, working here…it was too much, wasn't it?

She glanced at Sam and caught him watching the boys with a tender look she hadn't seen on his face before. Staying away from Samuel might seem the best answer for her, but was it fair to her sons?

Hannah let out a long breath as the decision solidified in her mind. "All right," she said.

Samuel stared at her for a moment as if not sure what she meant. Then a smile swept over his face. "Gut," he murmured. "Very gut."

Well, she'd done it. She'd committed to working with Samuel, seeing him regularly, letting him be part of the boys' lives. For good or bad, she was committed.

Chapter Four

"Settle down now." Hannah reached across the twins to be sure they were settled securely on the buggy seat. "You'll have plenty of chance to run and jump with Dorcas's boys when we get there."

She frowned at another wiggle from Will, but he had a quick explanation. "Elijah poked me."

"Did not," Elijah said.

"Did too," Will responded.

Hannah sighed. This seemed one of the disadvantages to having twins. There was no one who could be put in charge as the oldest. Will's ten-minute head start didn't seem to help, not like her two-years-older sister, Grace.

Will shot a guilty look at her. "Why aren't we going?"

"Are you finished being foolish?"

Both nodded, and Will leaned against her.

"Good." Suppressing a smile, she clucked to Ginger, and the pony trotted out to the lane obediently.

She'd seen her mother do the same in a dozen

different ways over the years. Whatever it was, Mammi didn't start until everyone was behaving. Even when she and her siblings were old enough to see what was happening, it still worked. Sometimes one of the kinder actually pointed it out.

They arrived at Dorcas and Jacob's house without further problems, and the boys came running out to meet them. The oldest, Timothy, took hold of the pony's bridle. "I'll take care of her, Hannah."

"Denke, Timothy." The two younger boys had already grabbed the twins.

"The barn cat is letting us see her babies. Komm, hurry."

They dashed off and Timothy, very aware of his superior status, took Ginger and the buggy off to a shady spot near the barn. Dorcas, emerging from the kitchen, welcomed Hannah with a hug and led her into the house.

"So, what's this I hear about you and Samuel making peace?" Dorcas asked lightly, lifting a steaming kettle from the stove and pouring water into the fat brown teapot.

"Not exactly that," Hannah said, wondering who had been talking about her. Most of the community, probably. "But with the boys inheriting half of the business when they're grown, it seemed best to compromise. At least Samuel seems good with the boys, but it's early yet."

"You'll keep an eye on him," Dorcas said comfortably, swirling the tea in the pot before pouring. "Maybe you'll find out you like Samuel better than you think."

"I doubt it," Hannah retorted. "Let's keep our adventure in matchmaking to the young people, all right?"

"Ach, it makes my stomach turn over just to think about it." Dorcas pressed her palm against her waist. "What if one of them falls for someone unsuitable?"

"Don't be silly," Hannah chided. "If there was an unsuitable person in that church, they wouldn't be in the group."

"I guess you're right, but there are always people who regret their choices when it's too late."

Was she talking about her and Jonas, Hannah wondered. Dorcas knew some of what had worried Hannah as a young married woman, but not all of it. She tried not to dwell on that. It hadn't been Jonas's fault that his troubles with his parents had affected their marriage.

"I keep thinking of what we were like at that age." Hannah could only hope none of the Pennsylvania teenagers were as strong-willed as they had been.

Dorcas shook her head. "At least our Katie is taking the whole thing as a big joke. She says she wants to have fun before she even thinks about getting married."

"Good," Hannah said. "She's one of the sensible ones, anyway. We shouldn't have trouble with her. Some of them…" She thought about the teens and twenty-year-olds who'd been at the picnic. "Some of them won't want to talk to us about what they're thinking. They think we're *old*."

She said the word with such disdain that Dorcas laughed. "Jacob says they have a lot to learn." Her face still lit with an inward glow when she said her new husband's name.

If she thought she could find Dorcas's happiness in a second marriage, Hannah decided she might be tempted. But it seemed so very unlikely. Besides, their project was to give the young ones more possibilities for good marriages, not to marry off the matchmakers.

"Well, we'd best get started on these lists for the weekend." Dorcas opened a fat notebook and spread some loose sheets of paper out between them. "Did you sign up to host anyone overnight?"

Hannah shook her head. "It's not possible. We don't have a spare cubbyhole big enough to take a bed since the boys and I moved back home. But my brother Thomas and his family did."

"Right. I think we're all set then." Dorcas shuffled the papers, counting them, and then they went on to the schedule.

They'd almost gotten through the plans for the weekend when they heard voices outside. It seemed that the boys were back.

"They are twins." Dorcas's youngest, Matthew, sounded as if he was trying to convince the others. "They are exactly alike. They even have the same white spot just above their noses. They're kitten twins, just like Will and Elijah are boy twins."

Hannah caught Dorcas's smile and they both listened, wondering what was coming next. "Well, it doesn't matter what you call them if you can't tell them apart." Silas, the next older one, sounded as if he were trying to settle an argument. "Anyway, they probably don't care."

"I don't know if kittens care," Will announced. "But I want people to call me by my right name."

"Lots of people don't." Elijah's gruff voice put in. "They think it's funny if they mix us up."

"We don't," Will said, and there was a note in his voice that hurt. Hannah wanted to rush out and remind them of all the things they liked about being twins, but she knew better. "Grossmammi and Grossdaadi always know," he continued. "And Mammi, for sure."

"Samuel always calls us by the right name," Elijah put in, and Hannah's breath caught. She hadn't noticed, but the boys had.

Dorcas nudged her under the table, and her expression seemed to say *I told you so*.

Hannah frowned at her. "It doesn't mean anything," she said, too softly for the boys to hear.

"Doesn't it?" Dorcas retorted.

She couldn't very well argue the point where the boys could hear. But she certain sure wished Dorcas would forget this idea she had in her head. She was giving every sign of matchmaking.

On Friday, Samuel left Joseph in charge of the shop while he headed out to the Miller farm. Annamae, the Miller family's youngest daughter, was one of the participants, and they'd offered to host the welcome gathering when the young folks from Cedar Grove came in.

Samuel would be meeting up with some of the other chaperones to get things ready for when the visitors arrived. And he'd also, if things worked out, be seeing Hannah and maybe even the twins, who'd been vocal about wanting to help decorate the barn for the event.

His friendship with Hannah was going better than he'd hoped even a week ago. She'd committed to a relationship that should allow the twins to learn about the business that would one day be theirs, but he suspected that one mistake on his part with the boys would bring that to a halt.

Turning into the long lane that led to the Miller farmhouse, Samuel promised himself that today, if possible, he'd tell Hannah about the deep regrets Matthew had experienced when it was too late to mend his relationship with his son. *If only...* Matthew had said that often after Jonas passed. Those had to be the saddest words a parent could say, he thought as he pulled up to the barn.

He'd barely had time to tie the mare to the hitching rail when Hannah's boys came running to meet him, both talking at once.

"We're going to decorate the barn," Will exclaimed, jumping up and down.

"Not just us," Elijah added. "Come and help."

They each grabbed a hand and tugged him toward the barn door that was pushed wide, with sunshine streaming in.

"Is your mammi here?" he asked, mindful of not starting anything without Hannah's permission.

"Right here," Hannah called, stepping into the doorway. "Come in. There's lots to do."

Pleased at the warm reception, Samuel let the boys pull him inside. Several people were working already—hanging paper streamers and attaching bunches of balloons to the posts.

Ephraim Miller was cautioning people not to leave any popped balloons on the floor, and he looked as though he was having second thoughts about having the party here. Nobody could guarantee to keep balloons from hitting the floor, that was certain sure. Ephraim was known to be very protective of his property. Samuel considered saying they'd be sure to clean up afterward but decided that might only make things worse.

Hannah was consulting with Dorcas over something, so he collected the twins to start on the decorating. Will came running with a roll of streamers and a pair of scissors in one hand and a bunch of balloons in the other.

Before Samuel could reach him, Will had started up the stall bars, discovered he couldn't climb without a free hand and slipped off the bar. Elijah, who seemed to be used to his brother's overreacting, snatched the scissors as Sam caught the boy.

His first impulse was to scold, but he swallowed the words. Matthew had scolded Jonas for every mishap, but it hadn't improved his behavior. Matthew had regretted that when it was far too late.

Will looked up at him apprehensively when Sam held him briefly against his chest. Then Will stared down at the floor. "I guess that didn't work. I didn't mean to run with the scissors, either. I was just excited."

"No, I guess it didn't work." Sam kept his

voice light as he put Will down. "You think it might work better if Elijah helped?"

Will looked at his brother. "Yah. Will you, 'Lige?"

Elijah grinned, and together they gathered up the streamers, balloons, tacks and everything else that had gone flying.

"How about if I reach up and you hand me the stuff?" Samuel stepped up onto the lowest stall bar while Will handed up the tacks and Elijah the hammer.

"Good work." He held up one end of the streamer. "About like this?" he asked, inviting the twins' opinions, but it was Hannah who answered.

"A little higher, maybe?"

Sam glanced the other way and found Hannah watching them, smiling. Some of the tension he felt in her presence had disappeared, and he found the four of them working together almost as comfortably as a family.

He backed away from that word. They weren't a family by any family tree, but the responsibility he felt for the twins had extended itself to Hannah. He hoped the opportunity would arise that he could tell her what had been in Matthew's heart. It might not change anything, but it would be the right thing to do.

Hannah left him with the twins and the decorating to help with the supper, and they continued to work with some fathers and children.

A little later, gazing at Hannah as she helped Dorcas's daughter Katie spread a cloth on one of the tables, it occurred to him how much she'd changed since the girl she'd been when Jonas wanted to marry her. That girl had been slim and quick and changeable, flitting from one thing to another and laughing all the time.

Now grief and responsibility had done their work, and Hannah was less likely to flit like a butterfly from one thing to another. Her figure was more rounded with maturity and her movements slower and more considered. If she were making up her mind about Jonas now, would her answer be the same?

Elijah said something to him, and he was glad to be distracted from that thought. It seemed a little lacking in loyalty, though he didn't know to whom.

"Grossdaadi is here to pick us up," Elijah repeated. "Come on, Will."

Simon Stoltz raised a hand in greeting. Will grasped his mother's skirt. "A little bit longer? Please?"

Hannah gave a light laugh. "And make supper late for everyone else? You know Grossmammi will have it ready when you get home, ain't so?"

"For sure," Simon agreed, drawing both boys toward him. "Tell everyone goodbye."

Obediently, they hugged both their mother and Sam and headed out to where the buggy waited. Samuel watched them walking with their grandfather, both chattering at once, eager to tell him everything that they'd done.

Hannah looked up at him. "What are you thinking about?"

He almost made something up, afraid that if he told the truth, he'd set a wall between them again. But the truth was the only way if she were to trust him.

"Thinking what a good relationship your daad has with the boys. And knowing that Matthew regretted not having his own relationship with the twins right up to the end."

Her face grew sorrowful, but at least not angry. "I always wondered why Matthew didn't try, at least after Jonas passed."

"Guilt," he said quietly, falling into step beside her as the bell on the back porch of the farmhouse began ringing. "He regretted the way they'd raised Jonas, with him too strict and his wife too lenient. He was afraid he might repeat his errors with Jonas's children."

Hannah froze, looking at him in disbelief. "Why…why didn't he tell me? We maybe could have worked it out together."

Sam felt some of the weight slide off his shoulders, and he could take a deep breath again. "Yah. I told him that, but he just couldn't seem to do it."

She gave him another searching look, and he thought he saw tears glisten in her deep blue eyes. Before he could think to say anything more, Bishop Thomas was calling them together.

As they moved more quickly, Hannah brushed away what might have been a tear and murmured, "You were a good friend to him, Samuel."

It was just as well that Dorcas and her husband joined them then, because Samuel didn't know how to reply to that.

Hannah stayed at the back of the group that gathered as the bus with the visitors pulled in, her thoughts in a jumble. If what Samuel had said was true, then she had misjudged her father-in-law, and she'd have to rearrange all that she had thought about him.

Oddly enough, she didn't really have any doubts about Sam. If he said that Matthew had been sorry at the end, then he meant it. Her throat tightened, and she swallowed back tears. What a waste that had been... If Jonas's father had really regretted the way they'd raised Jonas, being close to the twins might have given him peace.

The question was, would Jonas have been willing to allow that, if he had lived? She wasn't ready to face what Jonas might have contributed to the problem, and their visitors were piling out of the bus already, most of them stretching after the long bus ride.

Hannah forced herself to pay attention and shoved Sam's revelation to the back of her mind. He'd picked a difficult time to tell her about Matthew, but she had to admit that most likely there had been no good time.

The bishop welcomed the newcomers briefly and then called on Dorcas and Jacob to lead a few mixer games. She couldn't help but smile at the expression on Jacob's face. He'd been a serious, dignified businessman when he first came to town, but Dorcas and the children had changed all that.

Someone grabbed Hannah's hand and she was pulled into a circle by Katie, Dorcas's daughter. She seemed determined to see that everyone had fun, including herself. Well, Dorcas always said that meeting new people was an opportunity to turn strangers into friends.

Annamae, who was on Hannah's other side, looked as if she'd grab the first chance to run and hide. Hannah gave her hand a reassuring squeeze and smiled at the girl. Annamae managed to produce a smile, but at least she no longer looked terrified.

The game, under Jacob's direction, involved tagging someone you didn't know and then racing around the circle in an effort to get back to your space before the other person tagged you back. It didn't take more than a couple of rounds before people began cheering on the runner and chaser and a couple more before the group dissolved into laughter, chattering and giggling.

Dorcas didn't let the tempo drag, and after a brief pause for a drink and a snack, they were choosing sides for a volleyball game. Hannah tried to back away, but Sam chose her before she could escape. She went onto the volleyball court, making a face at him.

"I'll get back at you for this," she told him, but he just smiled, seeming to accept that as a peace offering.

She'd intended, in her turn, to pick Annamae, but when she looked, Annamae had vanished. Picking Katie instead, she resolved to find out what was going on with Annamae as soon as possible.

Then the game started, and she had to keep her attention on it. The kids, she decided, were playing harder than they ever had. Or maybe she just didn't remember.

She ran for a shot and missed, but Sam, coming in behind her, got it and set up an easy shot for her. Out of breath, she still managed to tip it over the net, and it fell between two advancing players. Satisfied, Hannah trotted off the court and gestured for another player to take her place.

At about the time it took her to pour a cold glass of lemonade, Sam came off the court behind her, face red and mopping his neck with a handkerchief. She laughed, holding her glass against her forehead.

"Are we getting old?" she asked, making him smile.

Sam poured his own glass and leaned against the table next to her. "A little, maybe. They aren't really better than we are, they're just faster."

"That's enough in a game like volleyball, ain't so?"

Sam's face was more relaxed than she'd ever seen it, and Hannah wondered if it was enjoyment of the game or relief at having told her about Matthew's guilt. Before she could frame a comment, he spoke again.

"It won't be more than a few years before Will and Elijah are wanting to play."

Hannah gave a mock shudder. "Don't say that. I'm not ready."

He chuckled. "You can't stop it, Hannah. They'll be asking to get a regular haircut and wanting to try driving a car. At least, Will would. I'm not so sure about Elijah."

She nodded, pleased by his insight. "How is it that you can tell them apart? Not many people can."

The lines around his eyes crinkled. "It's not so hard. Will has that little swirl in his hair at the top, and Elijah's eyes are a bit farther apart. And when they speak, it's easy to tell them apart."

Hannah was impressed. "Not even their great-aunt Ada can do that. Maybe you should give lessons."

He sobered. "I always wanted to be sure, so I've studied them since the first time you brought them to worship. Will had a blue blanket, and Elijah had a yellow one."

Startled, Hannah gazed at his face for a moment. He was serious. He'd taken a great deal of trouble to know everything he could about Jonas's sons.

"Why?" She asked the question before she had time to think about it. "I mean, why did you take so much trouble?"

He stared down at his shoes for a moment, and then met her eyes. "From the time Matthew took me on as an apprentice, I felt as if Jonas was my little brother. In fact, Matthew asked me to do so." He shook his head. "I don't know why. But it felt good to have someone I could think of as family. Especially after my folks moved out west."

Hannah felt as if she was seeing a different Samuel than she'd ever seen before. Without knowing quite why, she reached out and clasped his hand.

Sam froze for an instant, and then his fingers closed warmly around hers. Hannah's breath quickened. His hand was softer than she'd expected. Of course it would be, working with the oils that kept the leather pliant enough to work. She'd never noticed how warm his brown eyes were before, or how the wrinkles spread out from their corners.

How long they'd have stood like that she didn't know, but the game ended, and the teens came rushing to grab the jugs of lemonade and iced tea.

She slipped back a step, out of the way, letting her hand release his. What was happening to her? She was beginning to see Samuel in a different light, and she didn't want to change.

Chapter Five

Relief swept over Hannah as host families started picking up their guests. Dorcas, seeing her expression, chuckled and shook her head.

"You think we might be getting too old for this?" she asked.

"Definitely." Hannah had to laugh. "That's a sad commentary on us, ain't so? And my kinder aren't anywhere near the teen years. You're already there with your Katie."

"Don't remind me." Dorcas put her arm around Hannah's waist as if they were girls again. "At least this gang seems enthusiastic about getting to know each other."

Hannah's eye was caught by Katie, who was looking up into the face of one of the visitors, eyes sparkling, lips curving into a smile.

"I'd say your Katie is certain sure getting into the spirit."

Dorcas looked at her daughter and winced. "She's just like her mother was at that age. Jacob says if we get through her teen years, the boys will be a snap."

Hannah started to reply, but her eye was caught by someone who certain sure wasn't getting into the spirit of the event. Annamae stood back by the corner of the porch, and another step back would take her into the shadows.

Dorcas followed her gaze and sighed. "Any idea what's wrong with Annamae?"

Hannah shook her head. "I haven't had a chance to get her alone and have a conversation with her. Maybe now's my chance."

"I'll try to divert anybody who looks like interrupting you." Dorcas smiled. "Even if it's Samuel."

Wrinkling her nose, Hannah frowned at her. She'd had enough of people linking her name with Samuel's.

But Dorcas was already drifting away, so she moved casually along the fringes of the group toward Annamae, trying not to make it obvious. Whether she'd have succeeded or not, it seemed she wouldn't have a chance to find out. Annamae's parents were heading toward her purposefully, and Samuel was with them.

Hannah glanced at the spot where she'd seen Annamae, but the girl had vanished into the shadows. Frustration grew in her. What was going on in that family? At least it looked as if they were going to hear the parental view of the situation.

Hannah compared the three faces—Jane looked unhappy and reluctant in comparison with her husband, Ephraim, who was determined. As for Samuel...well, he just looked as if he'd rather be anywhere else. She tried to give him an encouraging smile, but he didn't respond.

Samuel started to speak, but Ephraim interrupted him.

"We have to talk to you. I told Jane we should have done it sooner, but she wanted to wait."

A glance at Jane seemed to say that she wasn't ready yet, but Ephraim wasn't going to be stopped. Annamae, Hannah remembered, was their youngest child, coming along years after the other children and probably getting more attention than she wanted.

"It's this whole thing about getting together with youth from another district," Ephraim plunged on. "Nothing wrong with that, I guess, but it seems to me we should let God decide who our daughter is meant for."

Was she confronting someone who disagreed with the bishop's recommendation? Hannah glanced uncertainly at Samuel. This might be better dealt with by the bishop.

"We decided about all that, Ephraim," Jane interrupted, her tone firm. "You agreed."

"All right, yah, I did, but I want it plain that Annamae should not use this as a chance to get closer to that Aaron Fisher." Ephraim glared at his wife, then at Hannah, who had a sudden desire to laugh but suppressed it.

"Ephraim, you agreed," Jane repeated. "Let me tell it."

Looking somewhat like a pony who was about to balk, Ephraim nodded.

"Annamae has known Aaron since they were little kids," Jane said, not looking at her husband. "It seems like lately they've been spending more time together."

Ephraim opened his mouth, but Jane pushed on. "We hope she'll make some new friends, that's all. She's a little shy and too young to be thinking about anything serious, anyway."

"So you just make sure she doesn't spend all her time with Aaron Fisher, that's all. Mind what I say."

Jane grasped her husband's arm, firmly turning him back to the group. "Komm. We must say goodbye to our guests."

"Not until I hear their answer." Ephraim planted his feet, reminding her more than ever of Ginger in a stubborn mood.

Trying to form an answer that might defuse the situation, Hannah found she was too late. Without a glance at her, Samuel spoke.

"We certainly won't do anything you wouldn't like," he said firmly. "You're the parents, and it's up to you to raise your daughter as you see fit. You can count on us."

Jane led Ephraim away, effectively cutting short the conversation. Hannah just stood there for a long moment, giving Samuel a look that should have knocked him back a few feet.

He didn't move, but he did blink. "What's wrong with you?"

"You, that's what's wrong with me." She had to force herself to keep her voice low. "How dare you speak for me? And what are you thinking? We can't act like guards, keeping that poor girl away from her friend."

"Don't be so foolish." He gave a quick look around, obviously thinking her voice might have attracted attention. "Her parents know what's best for her."

"Annamae isn't a small child. She's almost a grown woman…"

"Hush." Samuel grasped her wrist, but this wasn't the warm and supportive clasp she'd felt such a short time ago. "We can't talk about this here."

Unfortunately, she had to admit he was right. The group had dwindled, and folks probably could already see that they were arguing.

"No, we can't. But believe me, we're going to." She stalked away, wishing she'd never let her grandfather talk her into this situation.

* * *

Early the next morning, Sam headed for the Eshelman farm, where the community would join with their visitors in building a barn to replace the one destroyed by fire over a month ago. Normally he'd be looking forward to a day spent at hard physical labor with folks he knew in a good cause.

The cause was still good, but he suspected that before he could embark on the work he'd enjoy, he'd have to endure Hannah telling him how wrong he was about Annamae and her friend Aaron Fisher.

Not an argument. Disagreements with Hannah were too apt to accelerate into an argument, with both of them saying more than they should. Well, that wasn't going to happen this time, at least not on his side. He'd be calm, mature and soft-spoken, pointing out how wrong it would be to encourage these young folks to go against their own parents.

He realized his hands were tightening on the lines while his nerves beat a tattoo in his head. If he couldn't even think about it without getting agitated, it didn't bode well for his success.

Sam joined the line of buggies in the lane turning onto the Eshelman property. Folks were arriving already, despite the fact that the sun was barely over the top of the ridge. Maybe they felt the way he did about the day. But they certain sure didn't have his apprehension.

In another few minutes, he drew the buggy up next to the others in a long row. The younger of the Eshelman boys hurried along, helping to remove his horse's harness and hang it over the nearby fence. He exchanged greetings with those around him, relieved when a quick survey didn't show Hannah anywhere nearby. Good. Maybe he could get involved in the job before she arrived.

In another moment he heard the kitchen door slam, and a quick glance told him he'd been wrong. Hannah had just come out of the house. She stood at the top of the porch steps, looking around. She'd see him momentarily, but in the meantime, he enjoyed seeing her before she spotted him and her expression stiffened.

She wore a black dress, as usual, making him wonder how long she'd continue to cling to mourning. Black made her face pale, draining the color from it. His imagination gave him an image of her the way she'd looked when Jonas had been courting her. The peach-colored dress she'd worn then had brought out the peaches in her cheeks and made her eyes sparkle.

Well, she'd been a girl, whether she'd wanted to admit it or not. Now she was a grown woman, and her sorrows and responsibilities had weighed heavily on her. For a moment that dropped away as she greeted Dorcas and her sister, Sarry. Not wanting to be caught staring, he surveyed the gathering crowd, trying to pick out the visitors.

When he looked back, Hannah was still standing at the top of the porch steps. She had stiffened, and he knew she'd spotted him. He walked slowly toward her, eventually meeting up at the corner of the farmhouse.

"Looking for me?" he asked, trying to find a peaceful way of bringing up the subject that must be on both their minds.

Hannah seemed to disregard the question. "I said I'd start filling buckets from the pitcher pump so folks won't be traipsing through the house. Maybe you could help me."

He nodded, following her to the old-fashioned pump that had probably once been the only source of water for the farmhouse. He picked up a bucket and started pumping, leaving her to start the conversation. She didn't cooperate.

They'd filled two buckets before they both spoke almost simultaneously.

"About last night..." she began.

"You want to tell me how wrong I was," he finished for her.

"Not exactly." He received a chilly look from those blue eyes. "You were," Hannah said, "but I had no call to fly off the handle the way I did."

He was tipped off-balance for a moment, and

then he hurried on, wanting to take advantage of her unexpected admission.

"Then you agree that we can't help Annamae to disobey her parents."

"That's not the point," she said, sounding as if she too had vowed to hold on to her temper. "Anyone who looked at her could see that Annamae has been upset since this project started. I think we need to find out why before we get entangled with their troubles and do the wrong thing."

There was something to what she said, but the thought of interfering with other people's family troubles made him queasy.

"You wouldn't want anyone telling you how to raise the twins, would you?"

Of course she wouldn't. Satisfied that he'd brought up something she'd have to agree with, he set the next bucket down too hard and sloshed water over her shoes. "Sorry," he muttered.

Hannah frowned down at her shoes but seemed to brush off her annoyance. "When one of our brothers or sisters is in trouble, we can't ignore it, even if she is a teenager."

They were still on opposite sides. "She's a child," he protested.

"She'd old enough to start making decisions, even if she needs guidance. And if she doesn't get it, she's old enough to do something foolish that will affect the rest of her life."

Hannah almost looked as if she were talking about herself, and it sent a shock through him. Was she regretting what she and Jonas did?

Before he could say something that might make things worse, Hannah was going on. "All I'm saying is that we should talk to Annamae. And to the boy, too, maybe, but to Annamae first."

He drew a deep breath and then choked off what he was about to say. There could be no harm in talking, he supposed. If Hannah could ease the tension between Annamae and her parents, that was all to the good.

"All right," he said reluctantly. "But you'll have to do it. Annamae wouldn't talk to me."

Hannah's lips twitched at the idea. "No, she wouldn't. Then we agree? You won't say anything more about it until after I've tried to get Annamae to talk?"

"That's not quite what I said, but yah, I agree." He considered for a second and realized there was something more to be said. "And in future I won't try to speak for you." *Even if I know you're wrong*, he added silently.

"Good." She smiled, and he felt suddenly relieved.

Just one thing still troubled him. What had her expression meant when she spoke about making decisions one would later regret?

Hannah drifted toward the new arrivals. The air was filled with the buzz of conversation and intermittent hammer blows, but her thoughts were elsewhere. Overnight she'd been preoccupied with finding a way to work with Samuel, and it had even slipped into her dreams.

When she woke, one thing was clear in her mind. She couldn't expect him to be more rational unless she did the same. She had to stop flying off the handle with Sam. He'd called her impetuous, and he'd been right. Just exchanging a few words with him seemed to fling her right back into an eighteen-year-old again. *Impetuous* had been the word.

Once she'd had a husband and then two babies, she'd learned quickly that wouldn't do. She'd had to grow up in a hurry.

Maybe Sam had been thinking the same overnight thoughts, because he'd certainly been ready to listen to her this morning.

Now she had his agreement to her suggestion that she talk to Annamae. Her smile returned when she remembered his quick retort that she'd have to do it. It was good that he'd realized Annamae wouldn't talk to him. Hannah just hoped she'd be able to breach the girl's defenses. The sooner the better if she were to do any good.

Before she had a chance to look for Annamae,

the twins raced up to her, followed more sedately by her mother, carrying a basket probably filled with her donations for lunch.

Mamm looked around at the enthusiastic workers. "A wonderful gut turnout, ain't so?"

"It is. Curiosity about the visitors probably helped get folks here," Hannah added, making her mother laugh.

"I'll take these things into the kitchen and see what help is needed," Mamm said, already moving. "You boys be helpful."

The twins nodded solemnly, and Hannah could only hope that their help wouldn't be disastrous. Will was already tugging on her skirt, asking what they could do.

"All right, just listen." She started pumping, filling a pail to about the two-thirds level. After another look at her sons, she dumped a little of it out. "Most folks have taken a pail of water already, but it will be getting warm. The two of you can take turns carrying the pail and offering them a cold drink with the dipper." She put a long-handled ladle in the pail. "Take turns carrying, yah?"

Will grabbed the pail immediately. "I'll go first, right, Elijah? Later we'll trade."

Elijah considered for a moment and then nodded. "After each person we go to, we'll trade."

Will opened his mouth to argue the point,

then looked at his mother and nodded. "Okay. Let's go."

After three steps, they were sloshing water on their feet, but it was hopeless to try keeping them dry. She watched them approach the workers and then she started for the kitchen. Now to find Annamae.

A quick glance told her the girl wasn't in the kitchen. Moving casually, she walked toward the outbuildings, seeing what seemed like most of the teens and visitors. But not Annamae. Dorcas's girl, Katie, passed her with three eager young men helping her to carry supplies to the barn.

Dorcas's young ones had called Katie "Goldilocks" when they first saw her asleep in their barn when she'd run away from her guardian, Jacob searching for the woman she thought of as Aunt Dorcas. The nickname was well earned. Already a lock of golden hair had slipped out from under her kapp, and she pushed it back impatiently.

Hannah beckoned to her, and Katie veered in her direction.

"Having fun?" Hannah queried with a glance at Katie's followers.

Katie twinkled. "For sure. Can I do anything for you?"

"Maybe. Do you know where Annamae is?"

Katie was already shaking her head. "Haven't seen her for a while." Seeing that Hannah was waiting for more, Katie wrinkled her nose a little. "Annamae doesn't seem to be enjoying the visitors."

Hannah repressed a smile. "Not like you, ain't so?"

Again Katie twinkled. "Sure, it's fun. But Annamae is shy. She doesn't much like being around a bunch of people, especially ones she doesn't know. Want me to find her for you?"

Hannah smiled with relief. "That would be wonderful good. Just let me know where she is, okay?"

"Will do," Katie said. "Won't take long." She strode off, her followers trailing behind her.

Katie was as good as her word. Hannah had only filled another two buckets when the Unger boy, one of Katie's admirers, presented himself in front of her.

"Katie says to tell you over by the goat shed." He recited it like a lesson. "I don't know what it means."

"That's all right. I do." Hannah smiled. "Denke, Adam."

Looking relieved that he'd succeeded, the boy hurried back toward the barn, and Hannah headed in the direction of the smaller barn where the miniature goats were housed.

By the sound of it, Annamae must be hiding again, trying to avoid the crowd. So much the better for Hannah, if she could find a few minutes alone with the girl.

It didn't take long. Hannah rounded the side of the new barn, amazed as always at how fast a structure could go up when everyone worked together. She went on past the chicken coops until she came to a shed that housed the dwarf goats.

"Shut the door, quick!" The words startled her, as did the rush of a small creature determined to get out the door.

She grabbed the little goat by one horn and then wrapped her arm around its warm neck, avoiding the flying hooves. By the time Annamae reached her, Hannah was giggling helplessly, still hanging on. For a creature less than two feet high, it certain sure was a handful.

Annamae helped her wrestle the goat back far enough so that she could close the door, ending up on the floor herself. By the time Hannah pulled her to her feet, they were both laughing.

"Goodness, I'm sorry..." Hannah began, but Annamae managed, through her laughter, to shake her head.

"My fault. I said I'd let the goats out into the paddock. I should have opened that door before I let this guy out."

Together, they wrestled the excited goat toward

the back door. As soon as he realized where they were heading, he trotted along happily, reaching the door and then bolting out the instant it was opened. Naturally the others clamored to join him, so they emptied the rest of the pens and stood leaning against the door, watching the little creatures scamper around the fenced yard.

Maybe dwarf goats would be a good choice of project for the twins. She pictured Will wrestling with one of them. In a year or two, she amended.

Annamae glanced at her, drawing her attention back to the current problem. "You were looking for me, ain't so?"

"That's right." Truth was the only option, but Hannah knew she had to be careful, even though the goats had broken the ice. "I thought you looked as if you didn't want to be here."

"I don't." Annamae's cheeks flushed. "I'm sorry. I don't mean that the matchmaking project is bad. But I know what my daad is hoping, but that won't work."

That was more honest than Hannah had expected. "Do you want to tell me about it?"

Annamae shrugged, turning away a little. "You can't do anything. Daad is so stubborn..." She didn't finish.

"I know what you mean. Fathers are like that, especially with their daughters." If Samuel heard her, he'd have something to say, she felt sure.

Annamae hesitated, and then the words spilled out. "He doesn't want me to hang around with Aaron. Mammi said he told you that."

"Does that mean your mother doesn't agree with him?" This was getting more complicated by the moment.

The girl shrugged again, not letting Hannah see her face. "I don't know. Sometimes, I guess. But Aaron has been my best friend since I was a little kid. He lives right next door. Why shouldn't I talk to him?"

"Why do you think your father feels that way?" She was beginning to wish she hadn't started this, but Annamae clearly needed help.

"It's because of the spring."

Hannah blinked, thinking of daffodils. "Spring?"

"You know. Like that one." Annamae jerked her head toward a small cinder-block building that stood at the bottom of the hill. "We've always shared the springhouse, but when Aaron's father put a screen over the cistern without asking my daad, he blew his top."

Having had a glimpse of his temper, Hannah could believe it.

"The next thing Mammi and I knew, Daad was telling us we shouldn't have anything to do with them. And then Aaron said his daad felt the same way." She took a deep breath, and the words spurted out in a rush. "Aaron thinks we should run away together, but I don't want to do that."

"No, I don't think that would be a good idea," Hannah said carefully. Fortunately, the girl realized it. "Maybe you could explain to Aaron how you feel about it. If he cares about you, he should try and work it out."

Annamae just shrugged again, seeming to run out of things to say, but then added, "He's stubborn, too."

Hannah had an urge to shut them all in the springhouse until they could agree, but she squashed that notion.

"Tell you what." She put her arm around the girl's waist. "Will you promise me you won't run off without telling me about it and giving me a chance to help?"

Annamae gave her a long look, as if measuring how far she could trust her. "I won't promise, but I'll try." She pulled away, face set, wiping her eyes. "We better go."

True enough. It was nearly lunchtime, and Mamm would be wondering where she'd gone. She nodded and walked back toward the barn, hoping she hadn't just made a big mistake. After a moment's pause, Annamae turned away, apparently going to take refuge with the goats again.

Chapter Six

Hannah had a brief spell of relief after she left Annamae, quickly followed by guilt and apprehension. Annamae had unburdened herself, but she suspected that there was a great deal left unsaid.

Besides that, it was too much to hope that Samuel had not realized she had talked to the girl. He'd want to know how her talk with Annamae had gone. He wouldn't want to hear that the situation was even more complicated than they'd thought it was.

She hurried past the barn, aiming to offer her help in the kitchen, but before she got five steps in that direction, the twins rushed from the barn, calling her.

"Mammi, come see what we were doing." Each grabbed a hand and tugged her to the section of the barn where Sam was working.

"I thought you were helping your grandfather," she protested.

Samuel obviously heard that and shook his

head. "He turned them over to me. I guess what he was doing wasn't exciting enough."

"Have they been pestering you?" She'd hate to have him complaining about them or thinking she didn't know what they were doing. But all three of them looked happy, including Sam.

"Not at all." He tapped the two straw hats that bobbed around next to him. "They've been helpful...carrying and fetching and keeping me laughing while we worked."

Hannah couldn't help but smile at that. "Adding to your efficiency, ain't so?"

"I always work better when I have a cheering section. Right, boys?"

The communication between Sam and the boys was genuine, for sure. Why wasn't he married with kinder of his own? A woman couldn't help but approve of the tall, strong figure and deep, quiet voice.

"Mammi, you aren't paying attention. What are you thinking about?" Will tugged at her skirt. "I was telling you how we helped."

"Yah, I heard." But she could feel the heat rising in her face and knew that he was looking at her questioningly.

Fortunately, Elijah diverted their attention. He was standing on a stack of boards, looking up into the forest of wood crisscrossing the space above them.

"Aren't they scared?" he asked, watching men walk across the runners like walking on a field. "I would be scared. Would you, Sam?"

"I was the first time I thought about it." He knelt to bring his face level with theirs. "But my daad told me something that changed that." Both the twins were leaning toward him now, their faces intent. "Daadi said that we'd start at the bottom and work our way up, one step at a time. And that by the time I got to the roof, I wouldn't be scared anymore."

"Did it work?" Elijah asked softly.

"It did. A few days later we were there, and I stood right at the top when we finished the roof."

Elijah's apprehensive expression cleared, and he nodded, leaning against Sam's side trustingly.

Her thoughts repeated themselves. Why wasn't he married? Most Amish men were wed long before they reached their thirties, but there had never even been any rumors about Sam courting anyone. Wait, hadn't there been someone back in his teens? Maybe, but she didn't remember much about it.

It wasn't her business, Hannah reminded herself. She wasn't looking for a husband, and if she were, she wouldn't want anyone like Sam. She looked again at the twins leaning against him trustingly and felt a jolt. That trust didn't fit in with her opinions of Samuel. If the boys trusted him, maybe it was time she thought again.

"There's Grossmammi," Will said, instantly distracted. "Komm on, 'Lijah. She wants us." He grabbed his brother's hand, and they raced off toward the house.

Sam rose, watching them, and then switched his intent gaze to Hannah, bracing himself with one hand against the upright. "What about Annamae? Did you make any headway with her?"

She nodded slowly, trying to think of the best way to put it. Maybe there wasn't any best way. She'd have to tell him what the girl had said and hope he could see some way to proceed.

"She's very shy, but once she started talking, I think she was glad to have someone listening to her." She shook her head. "But I don't know what we can do to help her. It sounds like her father is angry with Aaron's father because of an argument about a springhouse they share."

"That sounds like nothing to have a quarrel with a neighbor about."

Hannah relaxed a little, her lips curving. "Yah, I know. Silly, ain't so?"

"There must be something more," he said, with the expression of a practical man faced with foolishness. "Are you sure she wasn't making it up?"

"I'm sure that's what Annamae thinks. I agree it doesn't sound like enough to cause this kind of trouble. It seems her daad told her she wasn't to talk to Aaron, but they've been friends since they were small children."

He shrugged, and she suspected he didn't know what to do any more than she did. "Ephraim has a hot temper, all right, but she's still his child. We can't interfere."

"She's not a child," she said impatiently. "Annamae said that Aaron wants her to run away with him." Remembering the despair in Annamae's eyes, she couldn't do nothing.

"We can't—" he began, glancing at the house as if looking for a way to escape.

"We can't stand back and let that happen. So don't keep saying we can't interfere." Her patience was slipping. "If young people that age feel everyone is against them, they'll just be more determined. I know. It happened to Jonas and me."

That brought his attention back to her in a second. "That's why this touches you so deeply."

She'd thought her words might make him angry. She certainly hadn't expected this gentle insight, and it left her speechless.

"Yah," she managed. "We can't watch this happening and do nothing." It wasn't easy to talk over the lump in her throat.

"Suppose we alert her parents..." he began.

"Then she'd never confide in me again."

"Maybe she confided because she wanted someone else to make the decision for her," he countered.

Hannah had to admit that he had a point, but she was afraid to take the risk. "She wouldn't promise to tell me if they were going to run away, but she agreed to try."

"What does that even mean?" Sam looked and sounded ready to give up. "You have two five-year-olds. I have no kinder. Why would anyone think we'd make good chaperones for a bunch of teens with their relationship problems? I've never been good with people issues."

His last statement had her staring at him. He seemed to mean it, but she'd never thought to hear him say so.

People were gathering around the tables now, and it seemed their time was up. She stopped, putting a hand on his arm to stop him, too.

"Please. At least let's agree not to do anything until we've talked again."

His frowning gaze studied her face, but finally he nodded. "All right. But it had better be soon—before anything bad happens."

A few days later that first matchmaking visit was over, and at least there hadn't been any explosions. Sam caught himself staring out the front window of the shop and turned away firmly, busying himself rearranging some bridles that didn't need rearranging. Just because Hannah was bringing the twins over today was no reason to hang on the window like some kid watching for his best girl.

He had to admit he'd been waiting for this day, but not necessarily eager for it. Hannah would want to talk more about the teenagers, while he'd be happy to ignore the whole subject.

Still, he'd committed himself to this project, and he wasn't a man to back out of his commitment. He glanced through the window again and then turned toward the machines at a word from Joseph.

"What was that?" He moved toward the older man, who was stitching the long lines of the pony's harness.

"I said, 'You're like a woman watching a kettle in hopes it will come to a boil.' Hannah won't get here any sooner by you watching for her." Joseph's eyes twinkled, and he wore a mischievous smile.

Sam had been trying to avoid Hannah spotting him. He hadn't thought about Joseph, who was always interested in what was going on.

"You do any gossiping about me and I'll put a bridle on you." Sam grinned, taking a threatening step toward the old man. Laughing, Joseph cringed mockingly.

"Anyway, you can stop watching." Joseph nodded toward the large windows in the front. "They're here."

Sam spun around in time to see Hannah handing a paper bag to each of the boys and then picking up a large basket before heading to the door.

He hurried to hold it open for them. The twins rushed in, both of them talking at once, vying for his attention.

"Hush, now," Hannah said. "You're making a racket."

"But Mammi, we're glad to see Sam," Will said, and Elijah added, "And Joseph."

"It's a good racket." Sam bent to greet each of the boys separately. Will's sunny disposition would carry him easily through life, riding its current, while Elijah's gruff little voice reflected more caution.

Will grabbed his jacket, tugging at it. "Grossmammi sent a rhubarb pie for lunch." He held up his paper bag. "And peanut butter sandwiches with marshmallow cream."

He tried not to grimace at the idea of peanut butter and marshmallow cream. It was a treat only a kid could love.

"I'm very fond of rhubarb pie. So is Joseph, so you'd better be sure to get a slice before we eat it all."

Will looked shocked for a second, and then he giggled. "You wouldn't do that."

"We'll be sure of it, ain't so?" Hannah hefted the basket. "Where can I put these things until lunchtime?"

He nodded toward the storeroom behind the machines. "There's a small cooler ready, if you need it." They followed him into the workroom, staring at the projects in different stages of completion.

"Do you have any plates and forks here?" Hannah looked around doubtfully. "I didn't think to bring them."

"Upstairs in the kitchen." He jerked his head toward the steps leading up to the apartment on the second floor. The bell on the front door jangled just then, and he turned back. "I'd best take this. Can you find your way?"

"For sure." Taking the basket and lunch bags, Hannah started up the stairs with the sure tread of someone who knew where she was going while the twins surrounded Joseph. They probably thought what he was doing was more interesting than waiting on a customer.

Sam had to agree as he helped two Englisch women who just seemed to want something Amish-made to take home with them. He glanced toward the stairs, trying to remember how neat he'd left the apartment. He wasn't usually sloppy, but...

He rang out the customers just in time to see Hannah emerge from the stairway, carrying some small plates and a handful of knives and forks.

"Find everything okay?" he asked, following her into the back room.

"Yah, for sure." She hesitated. "I did remember some things, though I haven't been upstairs for years. That wedding ring quilt is one that my grandmother made, isn't it? I saw her mark."

Ridiculous to feel embarrassed by the thought of Hannah checking out the quilt on his bed. "Yah, she did. It was when I was thinking I'd be married."

He stopped abruptly, watching memories chase across her face.

"I... I'd forgotten about it," she said, and a flush came up in her cheeks.

He carefully looked away. "Not surprising. Ella lived over in Riverport anyway, and you were very young." He was just as glad that Hannah didn't remember. It wasn't something to fill a man with pride that a woman would agree to his proposal and then back out a couple of weeks before the wedding.

Well, he'd learned one of life's big lessons

from that. He wasn't a good judge of people. He certain sure hadn't seen that coming.

"I remember my grandmother saying that..." She came to a stop.

"Go ahead," he urged. "Your grandmother is a wise woman, I think. And an outspoken one."

Hannah's color was still high. "She said that it was Matthew's wife who should have made your wedding quilt, you being like a son to Matthew. But she said it was no use expecting Matthew's wife to do something for anybody other than Jonas."

Before Sam could find an answer to that, the boys came hurrying over. "Joseph is finishing up the harness for Ginger, Mammi. Did you know that?" Will announced.

"He's rubbing it with neat's-foot oil to make it soft," Elijah added. "See? He gave me some." He held out his hand with a drop of yellow oil in it.

"Try not to get it on your clothes," Sam said, holding Elijah's hand in his. "If you rub it into your hands, it'll make your hands soft, too."

Elijah studied him for a moment as if to be sure he wasn't joking. Then he clapped his palms together and rubbed them vigorously.

"It works," he exclaimed. "See?"

"I want some, too." Will promptly ran back to Joseph, with Elijah right behind him.

"I'm afraid they're keeping Joseph from his

work," Hannah said. "They're good at distracting people. Maybe I'd better distract them."

Sam grasped her wrist, her skin warm and smooth against his. "One thing first. Have you thought about what we should do about Annamae?"

"I've thought," she said ruefully. "I haven't come up with any answers. What about you?"

"What about talking to the bishop about it?" Sam decided she didn't need to know that the idea had come to him just minutes ago. "He would keep our confidences." *And he's the one who got us into it*, Sam added silently.

Hannah seemed to consider his idea, her eyes serious. He could feel the pulse in her wrist beating against his palm.

"I guess so," she said at last, drawing her hand away slowly. "It really is a problem for him, since it's a quarrel between two members of the Leit that's causing the problem. Annamae and Aaron are just suffering for it."

"To say nothing of us," he added wryly. "This is beyond me. When should we see him? Tonight?"

She nodded. "Come to supper. I'll tell him we want to bring a problem to him."

"Won't the rest of the family want to know why?" From what he knew of them, they were all interested in each other's business.

A smile touched her lips again. "You could always want to check something about the harness, yah?"

"Actually, that's true. I'll bring it out and we can try it on Ginger."

Before Hannah could reply, the twins had burst into the conversation again, eager to put the harness on their pony and quick to assert their right to be first.

Sam saw again that calm patience that characterized Hannah's relationship with her sons. The impulsive teenager had grown into quite a woman.

If Jonas had lived, would he have matured as well? Or would he still be the irresponsible boy he'd always been? Sam would like to know what Hannah thought about that question, but he'd never be close enough to ask her.

As Hannah carried used plates to the sink that evening, her mother nudged her. "Are you sure Samuel doesn't want another slice of pie, Hannah?"

"No, denke." Sam reached over Hannah's shoulder to set down a pair of coffee cups. "It was delicious, but I couldn't eat another bite. We'd best get on with trying out the harness."

Hannah exchanged glances with Sam. No matter how delicious Mamm's peach and blueberry pie, both of them were eager to take their problem to the bishop.

"Us, too." The boys scrambled down from their chairs as Will spoke.

"We helped make it nice and soft for Ginger." Elijah rubbed his hands together, as if assuring himself that they were still soft from the leather oil.

"You can put it on the pony," Sam assured them.

"Go, go." Grossmammi waved her apron at Hannah. "I will help your mamm with the dishes."

Hannah shot a glance at her grandfather, and he nodded slightly, as if to assure her he'd be out in a moment.

She couldn't deny that speaking with Grossdaadi was the right solution. A problem between Amish neighbors rightfully belonged to him, but she still felt as if she were letting Annamae down. As if aware of her apprehension, Sam glanced at her cautiously. He didn't need to worry. She wouldn't go back on her word now.

She and Sam walked out to the barn with the twins running ahead. "Don't look so worried," he murmured as they went through the barn door. "It's the right thing to do."

She nodded, but a little voice in the back of her mind wanted to tell him that that was easy for him to say. He wasn't the one Annamae had confided in.

The boys were both trying to open the stall door at the same time, so she reached over their heads to pick up the crossties. In the few minutes it took for Sam to bring the harness and the boys to lead Ginger out, she had the ties ready to clip onto Ginger's halter, and Ginger rolled her eyes at Hannah as if annoyed at being harnessed up this late.

"It's your new harness," she told the mare. "You're going to like it."

"We helped make it for you," Will said.

Elijah, as if needing to set the record straight, added, "We rubbed in the oil to make it soft."

With Sam's supervision, they began to fit the harness in place, telling the pony that she'd like it and that they could go for a drive together. Hannah watched, smiling a little and wondering what Sam made of them.

When they were about to slip the headstall in place, Sam reached out to do it for them. Hannah intervened. "They should be able to do it themselves."

Sam's quick frown suggested that he didn't like to be corrected, but he handed the task over to the twins.

"Grossdaadi always says that you can't drive unless you can harness," Will said.

Elijah added, "And unharness, and wipe down the pony."

Sam nodded. "That's good advice, for sure."

He wasn't looking at her, and Hannah decided that if he was still offended by the correction, he'd just have to get over it.

But then he glanced at her with that quick curving of the lips that did service as a smile, and she relaxed.

The next half hour flew by as the twins took turns driving the pony cart back and forth on the lane while she and Sam watched. Then her grandfather joined them, watching as the boys came back with Will holding the lines.

"About time for these boys to get ready for bed, ain't so?" Her grandfather gave her a meaningful glance.

"Yah, I think so." She took the lines, and Sam held the pony's head.

"But Mammi, we didn't take the harness off, and hang it up, and…"

Samuel was watching her, probably enjoying her predicament.

"I know, but we'll have to practice that the next time," she said briskly. "You'll go in to your grandmother, because Sam and I need to talk with the bishop. Go on, now."

Sam nodded, as if admiring her poise, and he led the pony toward the barn.

Hannah felt tongue-tied at the prospect of telling her grandfather about Annamae and Aaron and their parents, but she was the one who'd talked to her, so she was the one who'd have to do it.

As they followed Sam into the barn, Hannah outlined her concerns about Annamae and the story the girl had told her. "We... Sam and I...felt that it was best to turn it over to you." She hesitated. "I hope you won't have to say who told you about it. I really want to help Annamae if I can."

Her grandfather studied her for a moment, and she felt he knew all the things she didn't say, even to herself.

Grossdaadi wiped the back of his neck with his handkerchief, something he always did when he was thinking over a problem.

Finally, he glanced from one to the other. "I should tell you that I'd already heard something about the problem from another source."

He didn't say who, but Hannah wondered if Annamae's mother had decided she needed help.

"I will be calling on both of them separately, and if I'm not satisfied, I'll insist on a formal visit with both men, taking along two other ministers."

Hannah's breath caught in her throat, and she exchanged glances with Sam. She didn't know what she'd expected, but her grandfather was taking the situation seriously. The steps he'd described could eventually lead to a ban.

"You'd best steer clear of that family until we're done."

Grossdaadi walked off toward the house, his head bowed and his back curved as if he carried a heavy burden.

"I know what you're thinking, but it's not your fault, Hannah." Samuel clasped her shoulder warmly. "It's where it belongs now, in the hands of the bishop."

"I know." Comforted by his gesture, Hannah nodded slowly and forced herself to look up into his face. "Did he really mean what he said? I still feel guilty."

His hand tightened a little. "Well, stop it. You must have an overdeveloped sense of responsibility for others."

"So do you," she said indignantly. "Or maybe it's your sense of duty that keeps getting in the way."

For a moment, she thought he would flash out at her with stinging words. But slowly his face softened, and his lips curved.

"We make quite a pair of chaperones, don't we?" He leaned closer, his eyes darkening. His head dipped, and before she could relax, his lips brushed against her cheek, and she stopped thinking anything at all.

Chapter Seven

Monday was predictable for Hannah, since it was laundry day, as always. But unlike most days, her thoughts were totally askew.

She stood beneath the clothesline, a sheet billowing in the wind, making no effort to pin it to the line. Until, that was, it fluttered right in her face. That jerked her attention away from those moments with Sam.

Pinning the sheet to the line, she picked up the next one, but even as she shook it straight, she was back in those moments with Sam. Now it was easy to think how she should have reacted. She should have shown him how shocked she'd been.

Unfortunately, she hadn't been shocked, or angry, or any of the things she should have been. Even now, she felt her cheeks growing warm despite the quick breeze. She could still feel the warmth of his cheek against hers, still feel the movement of his lips against her skin.

Hannah exerted all her concentration on making her mind blank while she hung the sheet and the last two pillowcases. It was unthinkable that she should react the way she had—leaning into his embrace instead of shoving him away from her.

Most embarrassing of all, Sam had had to be the one to pull away. He'd been the one to look horrified...the one to rush away.

Too late now. She couldn't go back and undo it. Snatching up the laundry basket, she propped it against her hip, prepared to go fetch the next load, when she saw the twins, carrying an egg basket between them, headed for the chicken coop.

She drifted after them, not wanting to interfere, but prepared to give them a hand if they needed it. Sometimes the hens were inclined to resent anyone who tried to remove their eggs, especially people they weren't used to.

"We didn't see Sam all day yesterday," Will was saying, and he sounded discontented.

"If was off-Sunday," Elijah reminded him. "We just saw Aunt Charlotte and Onkel James and their family. If we'd had worship, we'd have seen him."

"I know," Will grumbled. They moved along the nests, looking for eggs. "I wanted to ask Sam something."

Hannah had to bite her tongue to keep from asking what he'd wanted to ask, but fortunately Elijah asked it for her.

"What?" When Will didn't answer, Elijah nudged him. "Komm on. What?"

"You know," Will said. "About our daadi."

Elijah nodded his understanding, but Hannah nearly dropped the laundry basket. What on earth were they thinking? She was used to the fact that the twins understood each other better than she could have hoped to, but not when it came to Jonas. The twins had been almost three when he passed, and they couldn't have very strong memories.

"If Samuel knew Daadi well, then I thought maybe he'd think about marrying Mammi." Will's clear, high voice carried so well that Hannah had to look around to be sure no one else was in earshot. "I'd like to have a daadi."

"Yah. Me, too," Elijah muttered. "When I asked her about when we'll see Sam, Mammi said maybe we wouldn't go to the shop tomorrow."

"You shouldn't have asked," Will retorted.

"Nothing wrong with asking. You didn't want to."

"Yah, but if you hadn't asked, maybe she wouldn't think of it," Will snapped back, following it up by elbowing his brother.

A second later, Elijah returned the favor. The hens began squawking and the egg basket tipped dangerously. Hannah hurried toward them.

"What are you doing? You'll have those eggs

on the ground in a minute." Opening the door, she slid in. "That's not how you collect the eggs. You know better than that." She grasped the egg basket.

"Sorry, Mammi," Will said quickly, and Elijah nodded. "Sorry."

Their faces looked equally upset, and she knew she'd spoken more sharply than she'd intended.

"Ach, just think. We don't want to scramble the eggs before we get them into the kitchen, ain't so?"

They brightened.

"Go and check the rest, and let's get going." She gave them a gentle shove. "And talk gently. Hens don't lay well when folks are yelling at each other."

Whether that was true or not she didn't know, but she would think so. Thanks to the boys' squabbling, the hens were still moving restlessly and squawking every few minutes. The rooster, settled on the highest perch in the coop, glanced at them with what would be a disgusted expression on a person.

"We weren't really yelling at each other," Will stopped to explain, leaving his brother to search for the rest of the eggs. "Only Elijah said maybe we wouldn't go to the harness shop tomorrow, and we want to. You said we'd go on Tuesday and Thursday."

"Did I?" She couldn't possibly let them guess the reason for her reluctance.

They both looked at her hopefully.

"I just thought there might be too much to do here." That didn't sound very convincing. "We were thinking about making rhubarb jam one day this week."

Since neither of them cared for rhubarb jam, that didn't sound like a very exciting excuse. And her mother wouldn't care which day it was. "I guess we can do that on Wednesday."

Will bounced in excitement, and the red hen flew up right in front of him, squawking loudly.

"Sorry, Mammi." He ducked behind her.

"Get along out, both of you." She ushered them out of the pen, resisting the urge to swat the red hen with something.

She would see Samuel tomorrow. She would be calm and cool. It was Samuel's turn to be embarrassed.

Sam balanced the drinks in one hand and clutched the bag with sandwiches in the other. A few more steps took him under the roof that sheltered the entrance to the shop. After a sunny start, the rain had quickly changed the day to gray, almost silver where the drops glistened on the hoods of the cars along the street.

He headed to the door, feeling thankful for the

rainstorm. It had cut down the number of customers, and he hoped it would give him and Joseph a chance to catch up. They had too many orders and not enough helpers. The orders were normal when the weather got warm, since the Englisch horse owners were replacing gear and getting ready for the horse show season and Amish farmers were preparing for harvesting.

Not that he didn't appreciate the orders, but he had to face it...they needed another pair of hands in the shop. And he'd prefer someone who was either experienced or a quick learner.

As he reached for the door, a woman carrying a bright red umbrella ran into him, the umbrella catching his hat and sending it flying. He jumped off the step and grabbed it before the wind sent it rolling down the street. Turning back to the woman, he stayed where he was. If he went inside, Mrs. Everett would follow him, and then they'd never get rid of her.

"So sorry," she said, folding up her umbrella and shaking it so that the drops splattered on his shirt. "I saw you coming and just had to take the opportunity to speak to you."

Sam took another step back. He couldn't help it. Diana Everett was fairly new in town, having opened a women's apparel shop a couple of months ago. And she'd brought a lot of ideas with her from wherever she'd lived before.

She clasped his arm and stared at the bag from the sandwich shop. "You're about to have lunch, I see, but that's all right. I can talk while you eat."

Sam could imagine what Joseph would have to say to that idea. "I'm sorry, but that won't work today. Maybe another time." He made a movement toward the door, but she didn't release his arm.

"Oh, but this is so important. Summer is an important time for us shop owners, and we must take advantage of the tourists who come through. And that means special events. Now, I have an idea for each of the summer months—"

Sam pulled his hand free, nearly dropping the sandwich bag in the process. The woman would keep on talking for the rest of the day if he didn't do something about it.

"It'll have to be another day," he said, hoping he sounded sufficiently firm that she'd get the message. "I have some visitors coming this afternoon, and I can't lose any time."

At least he hoped he did. If Hannah and the boys didn't show up today, that would mean that he had ruined the plans Matthew had spelled out to him.

"But—"

"Another time." He stepped inside, flipping the sign to Closed and snapped the door lock. After all, several shops closed for lunchtime, even the pharmacy. He could, too.

"Looks like you have a follower," Joseph said, his eyes twinkling. "All the ladies like you, ain't so? Especially the Englisch ones."

"If you're trying to be funny, it's not working." He set the sandwiches and drinks down, managing to keep his voice light. Joseph's capacity for teasing him was never-ending. "That woman has lots of ideas but not enough common sense."

"Hannah has lots of common sense," Joseph said, starting his needle moving again.

Deciding it would only encourage Joseph if he said anything about Hannah, Sam decided to start on his sandwich before working on his next project. "What we need is more help to deal with the business we already have."

Joseph nodded in agreement. "Too bad the twins aren't a little older."

"Yah."

Would Hannah and the boys show up today? Or had he messed everything up? If she'd give him a chance to apologize...

He shook his head, thinking how unlikely that was. Besides, how could he ever explain his actions? He couldn't do that even to himself. For an instant, his skin tingled as if reliving the feel of her smooth cheek against his lips.

He had to get his imagination under control.

The bell on the door jingled. He stiffened,

not turning, hoping it was something that Joseph could handle.

Then he heard running footsteps coming toward the machines and spun around in time to field the boys, one in each arm.

"We're here," Will announced, and Elijah burrowed against his shoulder.

"I see that. We were just saying we needed some help around here, ain't so, Joseph?"

"Jah, for sure." He finished the leather he was stitching. "If you want to try the machine, I found some nice, soft leather for you to stitch on."

"Can we, Mammi?" The boys said the words in unison, and Sam finally managed to look at Hannah.

"If you promise to do only what Joseph and Sam tell you." Her voice sounded cool, but at least she was here. And talking.

"Let's go over here, to Joseph's machine," Sam suggested. "I don't want to stop in the middle of this."

The twins went at their usual speed, and he walked over behind Hannah. Joseph was already showing the boys the pieces of soft leather he'd found for them to practice on.

"Is that a special project you're working on?" Hannah asked.

He wasn't sure what she meant, but she nodded toward the project on his machine.

"Ach, no. Not exactly, but it's for a good customer, and we're getting behind with the work."

"Maybe I shouldn't have brought the boys today." She sounded a little uncertain.

"I hoped you'd come. With the boys, I mean." He rushed the words, then wondered why he sounded like such an idiot. "We decided that, ain't so? What we also need to do is get another leather worker, and I'm afraid the boys are a little young for the job."

As if to punctuate his words, Will ran his leather piece right off the work bench in his excitement.

Hannah relaxed, her smile returning. "I see what you mean. Is there no one in the area?"

"Nobody experienced."

She was looking at him, interested in the problem, he thought. This was probably the best chance he'd have to mend things between them, but he felt tongue-tied.

He cleared his throat, but that didn't bring any words to his mouth. "I have to apologize." He got the words out in a rush.

Hannah seemed to ignore his words. Instead, she was watching Elijah trying the machine. "You're sure they're not going to sew their fingers?"

"We haven't lost any fingers yet." He tried for a light touch. Obviously, she didn't want to talk about the incident. The only thing he could do was go along with her.

"That's how an apprentice learns. Listening to an explanation, standing beside someone doing it and then trying it for themselves."

The bell jangled again before she could respond, and two couples came in, middle-aged, the men carrying cameras, the women glancing around eagerly.

"Looking for souvenirs," he murmured, taking a step in that direction.

"I'll take care of it." Hannah caught his arm before he could move again. "You stay here with the boys." When he hesitated, she added, "Unless you don't trust me."

Unspoken was the reminder that she was trusting him with her sons.

"Yah, of course. Denke," he said quickly.

Hannah moved toward the front of the shop, not looking back. He turned to Elijah, who was waiting patiently.

He'd never understand women. But then, he never had, especially the girl he'd intended to marry.

Having often worked at her cousin's quilt shop, dealing with customers held no fears for Hannah. Sam had been right; they were tourists, and the women did want a souvenir to take home. Chatting with them, Hannah looked around unobtrusively for something that might be considered a souvenir. That was clearly not something that Sam had the time for. She fell back on the leather key rings, which seemed the only possibilities.

While the women were intent on picking out key rings, one of the men with the cameras edged over to her.

"I saw the sign outside about not taking any pictures," he began.

"We really appreciate your attention to it," Hannah said quickly. "Some folks just ignore it, and that's uncomfortable for everyone. Denke... thank you."

He looked gratified. "I wondered if you would mind my taking a photo or two of the things you've made. Our daughter loves horses, and I think she'd like to see them."

She glanced back at Sam, but he was fully occupied with the boys. "Yah, that would be fine." After all, Sam used photos for advertising, so he wouldn't object to this. "The saddles might interest her."

Hannah steered him over to the saddles at the front of the store, and he busied himself taking pictures of the various ones. A moment later he'd called his wife over, persuading her to pose for a photo of her sitting on the saddle. Their smiles and laughter were good to hear, and when they left, they'd purchased several key rings and two dog collars.

Hannah rang up their purchases, smiling. That should show Samuel that she wasn't entirely useless, even in a harness shop.

She tried to shake away the thought. She wasn't trying to get more involved with Samuel. After that embrace, the best thing was to stay away from him, but she couldn't.

He'd tried to apologize to her, but she hadn't let him. Her grandfather would not consider that appropriate. He would say it was lacking in humility. She probed her feelings the way a child would poke at a loose tooth.

The idea caused embarrassment, but pain? No, she couldn't say that.

Will and Elijah came running up to her. "We saw the lady sitting on the saddle," Elijah said. "Can we do that?"

She glanced at Samuel, who had followed them. "Did you ask Sam?"

"He said to ask you." Elijah glanced from her to Sam and back again.

"It's fine with me. But no running and no jumping, yah? We don't want to see you and the saddle on the floor."

They didn't wait to answer that question but scampered off to the saddle display.

"I hope that's okay?" She managed to look into Sam's face instead of past him.

"Yah, for sure. I don't think they can get hurt."

"Actually, I was thinking more of them causing some damage to the saddle."

His face relaxed in a smile. "If they could do that, it would mean we hadn't done a good enough job."

Something that was almost friendship seemed to move between them. Perhaps her grandfather had been right about the two of them working together. Holding a grudge against Sam did nothing positive for any of them.

An idea that had floated around in her thoughts came to the fore. "You were talking about the difficulty of finding someone to work with you. Would taking on an apprentice help?"

He glanced at the twins, and she laughed. "No, I don't mean them. You'd have to wait too long."

"Do you know anyone who might be interested? We'd be glad to have someone to train."

"Dorcas's oldest boy might be a possibility, I think. She was saying not long ago that Timothy hadn't decided which way to go now that his schooling is done."

Sam nodded slowly, seeming to go around all sides of the question. He would know Timothy, she supposed. Maybe she should have asked Dorcas before mentioning it, but it was a chance for young Tim.

Sam finally nodded. "Would you be willing to mention it to Dorcas? If the lad is interested, he could stop by and have a look at everything."

"I'd be glad to." She was getting to know Sam better...his way of looking at all sides of a question instead of jumping to an answer, like she did, for instance. And there was his surprising diffidence, as if he didn't want to risk being turned down.

She glanced at his face and realized he was watching her intently.

"Hannah, please let me say this. I'm sorry for what happened between us. I didn't plan it...it just seemed to happen."

"I know." She hurried on, as embarrassed as if she was the one who had attempted a kiss. "It's best forgotten, ain't so?"

She felt unable to go on, but Sam's gaze held hers. Finally, he nodded.

"I understand. I know you're not interested in anyone else after Jonas."

For a moment, the silence held between them. Then he went to collect the boys from the fascinating saddles.

Hannah stood where she was, repeating his last sentence in her mind. *I know you're not interested in anyone else after Jonas.* What had led Samuel to that conclusion? Was he right?

Chapter Eight

When she and the twins finally reached home and had taken care of Ginger, Hannah went straight into the kitchen while the boys rushed off to see what their grandfather was doing. She'd been gone so much recently that she felt guilty for leaving all the work to her mother. Not that Mammi ever complained.

After Jonas had passed, her parents had been eager to have her and the twins, only almost three then, back home with them. When she'd agreed, she'd promised herself that she wouldn't be a burden to them…that she'd do her full share of the work.

Back then she hadn't anticipated taking any part in the harness shop. She was still finding her way there, trying to decide what she could usefully do or if it was even desirable to get involved.

It was Jonas's legacy to his sons, she reminded herself. She couldn't just sit back and let Sam bear all the responsibility.

Hurrying into the kitchen, she found her next-older sister, Grace, stirring something on the stove. Grace's name was appropriate. She never let herself get ruffled and always had an air of quiet peace.

If people were like their names, she didn't know what that meant for her. Hannah in the Bible had been a patient woman, waiting to see what God had for her. That didn't describe her.

Hannah went over to hug her sister, taking a sniff of the aroma of the soup in the large kettle.

"Yum, smells good."

"Cousin Ada Ruth's seafood chowder. Mammi said she hadn't made it for a good while." Grace gave her a quick squeeze.

"True, but why are you making it here instead of in your own home?" She slid a strand of her sister's hair, the same golden brown as her own, back under her kapp.

"Am I coming apart?" Grace reached up to touch the knot of hair under her kapp. "That always happens when I'm cooking. And I'm here because Luke, bless his heart, took all the boys off fishing at Fulmer's Pond for the day. And he said they'd stop for a burger on the way home so I could have a day off from cooking."

"So you came over here to cook on your day off," Hannah finished for her.

Grace twinkled at her. "It's more fun than

staying at home all by myself." She gave another stir and turned the stove down. "Komm, sit. Let's have a cup of tea and you can tell me all about Sam and the harness shop."

"So that's the real reason you're here." Hannah lifted down the brown pottery teapot while her sister started reheating the kettle. "Curiosity."

"Just a little." She put mugs on the table, adding another one in case Mammi came in.

The kettle started whistling, and in another moment they were settled down with cookies and tea in front of them. Grace started to pour, and Hannah looked at her sister fondly.

As the only two girls in the family, they'd always been close, especially since there were only two years between them. She usually told Grace everything, even the things she hadn't told Mamm, and her sister did the same.

"So, the truth be told," Grace said, "I wanted to know how things were going with Samuel, now that you've decided to get involved in the shop."

"I don't know if that's the right word or not," Hannah said. "It's more like I've been pushed into it, starting with Grossdaadi."

Grace nodded. "Grossdaadi probably got tired of waiting. He likes to feel that everyone is settled." She frowned a little. "Including Samuel. How does he like having you and the boys intruding into his business?"

"Better than I would think. He's really good with the twins. I didn't expect that."

But Grace was nodding, unsurprised. "Because he's not married, I guess."

"Well, more because Sam didn't seem to think about anything but his business."

"The twins wouldn't let him ignore them, that's for sure," Grace said.

"Sam's about your age, ain't so?" Hannah eyed her sister thoughtfully. "Were you in school together?"

"He was a grade ahead of me. Then when we got into our rumspringa years, all the girls were crazy about him." Smiling, she seemed to be looking into the past.

"They were?" Hannah found that hard to believe. With that forbidding expression Samuel usually wore, she'd think the opposite would be true.

Grace nodded, wearing a reminiscent smile. "He was a different person then—popular, outgoing, fun to be around. You're wondering what changed him, yah?"

"Are you going to tell me?" she demanded. Grace could be maddening sometimes, especially when she knew more than Hannah did.

"It was about the time Sam's folks decided to move out west. Samuel was already an apprentice with Matthew's harness business, and he'd fallen head over heels for Ella Buckholtzt. He wanted to stay here, Matthew offered him a partnership and Sam's daaad put up money for the business."

Hannah nodded, thinking that was usual.

"So Sam proposed to Ella. His future was all set. Then, just a month or so before he and Ella were to be married, she broke it off with him. She didn't want to marry him after all."

Hannah was silent, thinking how hard that must have been for Sam.

Grace went on. "Her folks sent her down to Maryland to stay with an aunt until people stopped talking, Sam's family moved out to Indiana, and there was Samuel, left with no one."

"Surely he could have—" She stopped, knowing she didn't have any answers. What could he have done? "Sam mentioned something about his engagement, but…"

"It's surprising he even mentioned it," her sister said. "He never seemed to say anything. The way I heard it, he practically turned into a hermit, doing nothing but working. Matthew relied on him, especially after all that fuss about Jonas."

Hannah winced a little at that, and Grace clasped her hand. "Sorry. But none of it was your fault."

Wasn't it? Well, certainly not anything about Sam, but her marriage to Jonas was another story. If she and Jonas had been a little more mature, if Matthew hadn't been so determined to have his own way, things might have turned out differently.

She shook her head. She couldn't regret marrying Jonas, because the twins made all the difference. But Samuel didn't seem to have much consolation for his shattered marital hopes.

Grossdaadi didn't show up for supper, and Grossmammi was upset. "He said he had to talk with someone this afternoon, but he didn't say who." She covered a filled plate and set it on the back of the stove. "It's not like him to miss supper."

"Maybe whoever he was talking to invited him to stay for supper," Hannah's sister suggested. "I'm sure he'll be along soon."

Grossmammi ignored the suggestion as if Grace hadn't even spoken. "It's not like him," she murmured.

Hearing the clip-clop of horses, Hannah hurried toward the back door. "This must be Grossdaadi." But it wasn't. It was Sam.

Sam must have been astonished to see the whole family coming out to meet him. Grossmammi sank into the rocking chair on the porch, and Hannah stepped off the porch and put her hand on the front wheel of his buggy.

"Grossdaadi went out to talk to someone this afternoon. We expected him for supper, but he hasn't come back yet." She hesitated and then went on. "Why have you come?"

She realized that sounded unwelcoming but was too concerned to rephrase it.

Sam picked up on her concern. "He left a message on the shop phone and asked me to come over." Sam's voice lowered. "He said he wanted to talk to us again about…the situation."

"I'll go out to the road and see if he's coming," she began, but Sam reached out a hand to her.

"We'll both go," he said.

The boys, searching for ripe strawberries, seemed to realize something was happening, and they ran toward the buggy as Hannah clasped Sam's hand and Sam pulled her up to the seat.

"Can't we come?" The twins spoke in unison, but Hannah shook her head.

"You stay here and help your grandmother. We won't be long." Before anyone could shoot questions at them, Sam was turning the buggy and starting out the lane toward the road.

But not far—only a few yards down the lane they saw her grandfather's buggy coming toward them. Sam pulled to the side and jumped down, tossing the lines to Hannah, and she quickly saw why. Grossdaadi leaned forward, his face gray, the lines limp in his hands.

She jumped down and ran over, reaching up to clasp her grandfather's hands. "Grossdaadi, are you all right? What happened?"

He shook his head slowly, and she wasn't sure he heard or understood what she was asking. A wave of panic ripped through her.

Meanwhile, Sam swung himself up next to the older man, putting a supporting arm around him. "Let's get him back to the house. He's maybe had too much sun."

That was a reasonable explanation, but Hannah's mind flew to her grandfather's determination to see Annamae's father and find out about his discord with his neighbor. That was probably where he'd been.

She turned the other buggy, following Sam back to the house, her thoughts jumping from questions to prayers. As they drew in, her father came hurrying to meet them. Mammi put her arm around Grossmammi and Grace held the door open. Making a chair with their hands, Sam and her father carried Grossdaadi inside quickly. Handing the two buggies over to the twins to tether the horses, Hannah hurried into the kitchen.

Grace was already wringing out a soft dish towel with cool water. Grossdaadi murmured that he was all right.

"Ach, don't you tell us that." Grossmammi's

color came back as she held a glass up to his lips, her fear emerging in scolding. "You were doing too much today, running around in this hot weather. You should know better."

He tried to protest, but she grabbed the wet cloth and began sponging his face, pressing him back in the chair.

The twins slid in the screen door, sidling over against the wall and staring, their eyes huge.

Grossdaadi, as if suddenly aware of his audience, struggled to sit up straight, only to be pushed back again, gently but firmly.

Grossmammi, clearly in charge, spoke with sudden decision. "You'll lie down and be quiet for a bit. That's what you need." She looked from Daad to Sam. "You'll move him to the sofa in the grossdaadi haus, yah?"

Nodding, they moved to either side of him. Bypassing any argument about his walking, they each took one side of the chair, as if they'd planned it out. In a few moments they had vanished into the other side of the house.

Hannah took a step after them, but Mamm shook her head. "Let your grandmother settle him. I'll check in a moment and see if she wants anything."

It would be easier, Hannah decided, to be busy. The table was already set, but she stirred the chowder on the stove to keep it from sticking.

Nobody would want charred soup, and Grace was cutting a fresh loaf of bread.

When her father and Sam came back in, Daad was quickly reassuring. "He looks better already. It must have been doing too much and the heat of the sun, like Grossmammi said."

Hannah found herself exchanging looks with Sam. They knew a little more about it, and she wondered if Sam felt as guilty as she did.

Sam stood awkwardly by the door. Obviously, he wouldn't be talking to the bishop today, and the fact that the older man had wanted to talk to him and Hannah surely indicated that things weren't going well.

Hannah's mother started dipping up chowder into bowls. She paused, looking at him. "You'll stay for supper, yah, Samuel?"

"That's kind of you, but I can't. Whatever the bishop wanted to see me about will have to wait until he's feeling better, so I'd best get back to work."

"You can take some chowder home with you," she suggested, taking a quart jar out of one of the cabinets. Obviously, like a lot of Amish women, she hated to let anyone get away without eating.

"Denke. Another time." He lifted a hand in farewell. "I hope he'll soon be well."

He glanced at Hannah, thinking he'd say goodbye, but she shook her head. "I'll walk out with you." She grabbed the handle of the screen door and followed him outside.

"It wasn't just the sun," she said urgently. "Something else must have gone wrong."

His horse was tethered to the hitching rail where the twins had left him. He stopped, lifting his hand to the seat and nodding slowly. "You don't know that, but looks like it."

Hannah's blue eyes grew brighter when they filled with tears. "Maybe it was our fault. Maybe we shouldn't have told him."

She looked so bereft that he had to clasp her hand. "You know what he'd say to that, ain't so?"

Hannah managed a faint smile. "Yah. He'd say it was the bishop's responsibility."

"Nobody but God can take that away from him. We all know that's true." The drawing of the name of a new bishop was a solemn event, and no one who had gone that far had ever turned back from the challenge.

Sam knew more about that sort of responsibility than Hannah ever could. His responsibility to Matthew had cut him off from being a help to Hannah and Jonas.

"Sometimes being responsible for someone can go wrong. The Lord knows it did for me," he said, half to himself.

He'd tried to do his best, to repay his debt to

Matthew and to help Jonas to a better relationship with his father, but he had failed.

"Now that's not right and you know it." She was scolding him...gently, but it was scolding. "You don't know what the Lord has planned for anyone else, and sometimes even for you."

"Yah, but..."

"But if you're talking about me and Jonas, you'd best forget it. Whatever was good or bad about our marriage, we had the twins. I wouldn't trade them for all the happy endings in the world."

"I know, I know." He held her hand cradled in his, and she made no attempt to pull it away.

Hannah said, "I never understood why Matthew didn't want me to marry his son, but that's all in the past."

His fingers tightened on hers as he stared at her. She had it all wrong. "It wasn't that he didn't approve of you, Hannah. It was because of Jonas. He believed Jonas wasn't grown-up enough for marriage, and he feared he never would be."

There was silence between them, laden with questions, regret and pain.

Hannah shook her head slowly. "I don't understand. You must be wrong. How could he think that about his own son?"

"Because it was true...or at least, he was convinced it was. Matthew felt that his wife had spoiled the boy so that he'd never truly grow up. And Matthew felt that he had failed as a father…trying to counteract the harm he thought she had done."

Hannah was quiet, not looking at him. Then she looked up, and he realized there were tears trickling down her face.

"Don't," he said softly, brushing a tear away.

"It's so sad." Her voice was choked with feeling. "I didn't realize." She turned her hand so that she was clasping his. "It wasn't your fault, Samuel. No one blames you."

No. Only himself, it seemed.

Her lips curved in a smile, even as her eyes still glistened with tears. "I'm glad you told me."

If he looked into her face any longer, he would take her in his arms.

He loved her. The realization hit him like a bolt of lightning. He loved her, and he couldn't tell her. He had already messed up her life once. He couldn't possibly risk doing it again.

Chapter Nine

As Hannah went into the twins' bedroom, she tried to dismiss from her mind everything that Sam had said about Jonas and his father. The boys wouldn't understand any of that, because nothing in their short lives had prepared them to understand.

She wasn't sure that she understood it herself. How could a father let such a distance grow between him and his child?

The boys slept in the twin beds that two of their uncles had once used, but neither one was sleeping. Will, in fact, was sitting on his pillow, bouncing a little, while Elijah burrowed under his.

"That's no way to fall asleep," she said lightly, pulling Elijah out from under the pillow. "What's up?"

Elijah wrinkled his nose. "I didn't want to listen to Will any longer."

"Why not?" She settled him into his bed and tucked the patchwork quilt around him. They both claimed they couldn't go to sleep until they were tucked in, and she could feel him relaxing from the slightest touch.

"He was talking about..." Elijah stopped, exchanging glances with his brother.

"You were worrying about your great-grandfather, yeah?"

They both nodded solemnly.

"I'm sure he's going to be all right by tomorrow," she assured them. "He just needs to have a good night's sleep."

At least, she hoped that was true. Her grandmother knew him better than anyone, and she'd be watching him all night, if Hannah knew anything about it.

The twins seemed reassured, so she left it at that, trusting that they hadn't picked up on her own concerns. If only she hadn't told her grandfather about the problems between Annamae's father and the neighbors.

But Sam had been right about it. That was a problem that belonged to the bishop, not to them.

"Now, how about a story?" She shook up Will's pillow and pushed him gently into place. "One of your books?" She glanced at the shelf between the beds, which held a battered collection of their favorite stories.

"Tell us a story about our daadi," Will said

quickly, and Elijah nodded. Clearly, they had decided that together.

"All right. What kind of story?" Hannah found she was wondering about that request. Were they conscious of how little they remembered about Jonas? Maybe they were trying to fill those blanks in with stories from his childhood.

"Tell us about a time he got into trouble." As usual, it was Will who plunged in.

She glanced at Elijah to find him nodding.

"All right. Let me think for a minute." Jonah had certain sure gotten into trouble enough, and as his childhood friend, she'd heard about most of those times.

"Well, there was the time that he tried to climb up the windmill. I told him he'd get into trouble, but he thought it would be fun to be up so high." Once she'd started the story, she realized that this was a story that involved Samuel coming to the rescue.

"What happened?" Will's eyes were wide. He didn't like being up high. Maybe this wasn't a good story to pick. She'd best shorten it.

"Go on, Mammi." Elijah nudged her.

"He got up above my head, and I told him that was far enough. It made me dizzy just looking up at him. He tried to climb up one more step, but he missed."

"Did he fall?" Will whispered.

She shook her head quickly. "He held on with one hand. He was laughing, but then his hand started to slip."

She could still feel the cold sinking in the bottom of her stomach. Both boys were staring, wide-eyed. They didn't understand that Jonas had always wanted to do whatever anyone told him not to. Thank goodness they hadn't inherited that from their father.

Hannah put one hand on each of them. "So, then Samuel came running. I don't know how he knew. He pushed past me, and I sat down, scared to look."

"Samuel saved him, ain't so?" Elijah said.

"That's right." The sooner she was out of this story, the better. "Samuel saw what was happening and swarmed up the ladder like a...a monkey," she said, reminded of the storybook they loved.

"Sam grabbed him and brought him down, right?" Will said, bouncing in excitement.

"That's what happened, yah. He grabbed him by the seat of his pants and lifted him down to the floor. Now get back under your covers."

They slid down obediently again, and she tucked each of them in again. Bending over, she kissed Will's cheek while he gave her a throttling hug. She loved these moments at the end of the day, loved tucking in her two sweet boys.

By this time Elijah's head was back under his pillow, but she could see his eyes peeking out. She kissed his ear, and he turned to hug her.

"Good night, sleep tight," she whispered, and they closed their eyes.

But as she stood, Will's eyes popped open again. "If we ask Samuel, will he tell us some more stories?"

"I don't know." The key was to keep walking toward the door, not letting Will think he was delaying her. "You could ask him." She switched off the light and slipped out, breathing a sigh of relief.

Pausing for a moment at the stop of the stairs, the thing Sam had said about Matthew's reason for opposing their marriage came out from its hiding place. Oddly, she hadn't doubted for a moment that Sam was telling the truth.

She had told herself that she had forgiven Matthew, and here was yet another reason why that forgiveness was needed. She should be happy. Hannah leaned her head against the wall for just a moment, trying to sort out her thoughts.

She had been blaming Matthew, but if she couldn't blame him, who was to blame for her hasty marriage? Samuel? He'd just been trying to rescue Jonas, as he had that day on the windmill. That left only Jonas. And her.

Hannah pushed that thought away, but it clung

like a tick. She had given in to Jonas's determination to marry, hadn't she? Jonas had been immature, but she had been, as well. Getting married had seemed such a grown-up thing to do. She shook her head at the girl she'd been then. If she'd been a little older, a little wiser, would she have seen that they were both too young?

She sucked in a deep breath and started down the steps. It was too late to change anything about it. An image of Annamae slid into her thoughts. If she could stop her from making a mistake, that would be a blessing.

No one had stopped her and Jonas from marrying, and she had to admit that there had been moments she wished they had.

No, she couldn't...didn't...wish that, because their marriage had given her the twins to love and raise. That was worth anything.

Busy as usual the next morning, Samuel was bending down checking the showcase for the number of bits on display when Joseph called out.

"Look who is here. Were you expecting her?"

Samuel emerged from behind the counter to find Hannah just coming in. His first thought was concern for the bishop. "Is something wrong?"

"No, no," she said quickly. "He's much better this morning, but my grandmother is insisting he spend the day in his chair." A smile lit her face, chasing away the somber look she'd worn. "We'll see how long she succeeds in keeping him still."

"Not an easy job, yah?" He moved to meet her, keeping himself from reaching for her hand. "You wanted to see me?"

That was a little hard to believe, he thought.

"Grossdaadi said I should come and tell you what happened with Annamae's family yesterday. And there was something else I thought we should talk about before the boys are here again."

He nodded, wondering if he'd done something wrong. Or if she thought he had. "Let's go back and have some coffee. Joseph just made a pot."

Hannah paused in midstep. "He'll want a cup," she began, and Joseph, eyes twinkling, started to rise.

"I'll bring it to him," Samuel said firmly, steering her to the back of the shop. While she took a seat at the small table, he filled three mugs and carried one out to Joseph, who still looked amused.

Hannah, holding her coffee, was looking at the list of projects due that was tacked to the bulletin board. She stepped away when she realized he was there.

"Sorry. I didn't mean to be nosy."

"Ach, don't be silly. Everything here is half yours, anyway."

She shook her head, coming back to the table.

"Anyway, Grossdaadi wanted to thank you for your help yesterday." She went on before he could say that he hadn't exactly been a lot of help. "His talk with Annamae's father didn't go well. He said he guessed Ephraim Miller must be about the most stubborn man he'd ever run into."

Sam nodded, taking a sip of his coffee. "He's one who will count up the wrongs he thinks others have committed against him."

He'd had a round or two with the man himself, and at one point he'd thought about telling him to take his business elsewhere. A person couldn't do that with a brother in faith, no matter how justified he felt.

"Grossdaadi said as much, and he never does say anything bad about anyone. Anyway, my grandfather feels it will mean a call on Ephraim Miller again and maybe his neighbor by him and the ministers. But that doesn't have anything to do with us," she added hurriedly.

"No, except that it might make things worse for those children."

She nodded, lines tightening around her eyes. "Poor Annamae. I'm afraid they might be so foolish as to run away."

"That would for sure bring it out in the open." He'd never claimed to be an expert when it came to teenagers, and his one experience with Jonas hadn't worked out very well.

Still, Hannah was looking at him as if hoping he'd come up with an answer. "If you could get Annamae talking to you again, that might help."

"Yah, but how? Ephraim wouldn't look kindly on any of the bishop's family, I suppose."

Hannah's caring was written on her face. So caring, and so eager to help. If anyone could, it was surely her. Her fingers were wrapped around her mug, and he had to resist the impulse to touch her in sympathy.

"Is there anything you could ask her to help you with? Watching the boys, maybe, or something in the garden."

"Asking her to watch the twins probably wouldn't give me much chance to talk quietly with her." Her lips twitched. "But actually, it might be helpful to have an extra pair of hands when we're canning rhubarb. Seems like with rhubarb you either don't have any or it overflows. This is one of the overflowing years."

He nodded slowly. "Good idea, but what if Ephraim says no, since it's you asking for help?"

"I'd just check with Dorcas for something like that. She'd probably be glad to have a batch of canned rhubarb sauce or jam. I'm pretty sure she doesn't grow any." The confidence had come back into her voice.

"Denke, Samuel." She reached out and put her hand lightly on his wrist. "That was a gut idea."

He tried not to think about the warmth from her fingers traveling right up his arm to his heart. He cleared his throat and drew his hand away reluctantly.

"You said there was something about the boys..." he said.

"Ach, yah." She flushed, the color coming up in her cheeks. "They asked for a bedtime story last night about their daadi, and I told them about the time Jonas climbed on the windmill and you rescued him. So now they're going to ask you to tell them more about Jonas when he was a little boy. I thought I'd better warn you."

Even as he nodded in response, his thoughts went back to the Jonas of those days, the small boy who followed him around and wanted to do exactly what he did. Jonas had been the little brother he'd always wanted. It was painful to think of how that had changed...how he'd been caught between his affection for Jonas and his duty to Matthew.

The repercussions from that were still echoing in his heart, keeping him from expressing his feelings for Hannah. He was caught, and he didn't see any way out.

Hannah sat for a moment, idly looking around the back room...part office, part workroom. Bits of leather lay here and there on the floor, but tools hung in an orderly progression from the wall above the workbench.

What did the space tell her about Samuel? For sure it said that he loved his work. Even in a moment of idleness, his right hand caressed a scrap of leather, the fingers smoothing it out and then curving it around.

She'd expected more of a response to a request for him to talk to the boys about Jonas, but he'd said very little. He stared at the cup of coffee he held, seeming unaware of it.

The lines of his face reflected loss, she thought, as well as determination to do what he felt was his duty, even when it pained him. Then, as if he felt her studying his face, he glanced up, shook his head and rose, carrying the cup and spoon over to the small sink in the corner.

"I'd best get back to work. I'm behind on a project for a good customer."

Hannah nodded, carrying her own spoon and cup to the sink and following him out into the shop. "Yah, me, too. I have to pick up some things for Daad at the hardware store." But she hadn't finished all she wanted to accomplish without the boys here.

She stopped by the counter, and he stopped with her. She said, "I noticed that you were working on your display…or maybe inventory. I wasn't sure what, but it seemed to me a shame that you had to spend your time on that when you need to be working on the leather goods."

Samuel shrugged. "It has to be done. It's part of running a business."

"Yah, but...well, Daad always says it's better to do what no one else can do, even if you have to pay someone for the other things."

"I suppose." He seemed to be hiding behind his impassive expression, and she wondered if he thought she was butting in where she didn't belong.

There was no point in leaving it at that. "Why not let me do that sort of thing? When I bring the boys in, there's no sense in my doing nothing. I could take care of stocking shelves or keeping records."

He seemed to process her suggestion, and she had to remind herself that was his approach to anything new—to walk all around it and consider it carefully.

Finally, he made a dismissive gesture. "You don't need to do that, Hannah. We can manage."

"I'm sure you can, but I don't like to be idle. I agree it's a good idea for the boys to get used to the business. If half of it is going to belong to them one day, then I should be a part of it."

She was tempted to add that if he didn't want her around to just say so, but she managed to restrain herself. But what was so difficult about her proposal? It wasn't as if she wanted to interfere, was it?

"Are you sure? Jonas didn't want anything to do with the business."

"And you thought I would automatically feel the same?"

"You did at first, ain't so?" His eyebrows lifted slightly, questioning her, and she knew she had to answer honestly.

"Yah, I did, at first. When I was a newlywed. But I'm a little older now, and maybe a little wiser. Maybe, if Jonas had lived longer, he'd have changed his mind, too."

Not that Jonas had been likely to change his attitude toward anything. He jumped from one enthusiasm to another, and if that didn't work out, he dropped it. But he had never had anything good to say about working in his father's business.

She shrugged, smiling a little. "Someday I hope that one or both boys will want to take part in the business their grandfather started. That's what Matthew wanted, ain't so? It's only common sense to give you a hand when I can."

If that didn't convince him, she didn't know what would. She moved a little impatiently. "If you don't want me to be involved, just say so." There was a bit of a snap in her voice.

Samuel's face relaxed, and his lips curved.

"Always in a hurry, ain't so? If you're sure, I'd be glad to have you help here, Hannah. Whenever you want."

"Gut." She gave a short nod. "I will see you tomorrow, then."

She went out quickly. Each time they talked, it seemed she was showing more of her feelings to Samuel. Maybe that was wrong, but she couldn't help it. What would Jonas have thought of that?

If you love me, you'll be on my side. That was what Jonas had said when she'd suggested that they could wait a bit before marrying. She had a vivid memory of Jonas clinging to her, begging her not to let anyone tear them apart.

She hadn't been able to say no, not when he needed her so much. Now it was the twins who needed her, and no matter what, she would do what was best for them.

Chapter Ten

Hannah picked up a large plastic pail and a sharp knife and followed her mother toward the rhubarb patch. A quick glance down the lane told her Annamae wasn't in sight yet.

Mamm caught her glance. "Worried?"

"No, not exactly worried. I should be figuring out how to convince the girl that running away isn't the answer, but I can't. Every time I try to find the words, I keep thinking about Jonas." She tilted her face toward the sky, enjoying the warmth of the sun on her skin and trying to clear her mind.

"Ach, that's not surprising." Her mother sounded gently confident. "Annamae's problem reminds you of what happened with Jonas, ain't so?"

"I guess." She wasn't sure about that...or about a lot of things. "I suppose it is similar, except that Jonas finally got what he wanted without running away."

"Just Jonas?" Her mother asked, an odd note in her voice.

"Both of us, I mean," she corrected hastily. "When you and Daad agreed, then Matthew gave in. But I still always felt he disapproved of Jonas marrying me."

Samuel had said it wasn't that, but she didn't see how Samuel could be sure.

"Matthew thought you both were too immature to make that decision." Mamm almost sounded as if she had agreed with him.

"Maybe we were," she admitted. "And Annamae is even more immature than I was then. I don't want to see her make a mistake." She almost added, *like I did*, but thought better of it.

They'd reached the first row of rhubarb plants, the big leaves like elephant ears shielding the ground beneath. Bending, she pulled one of the ruby stalks and then cut off the leaf, letting it fall under the plant while she dropped the stalk in the bucket. She glanced at her mother to see that she was several stalks ahead of her.

"We thought long and hard about our decision," Mamm said, staring down at the rhubarb stalk she held in her hand. "But we were afraid of losing you altogether if we didn't let you marry."

Hannah thought back to the image that had popped into her mind...of Jonas, eyes filled with tears, begging her not to let anyone come between them.

"And I was afraid of losing Jonas. And now

Annamae is afraid of losing Aaron. Marrying shouldn't be about being afraid, should it?"

Her mother gave her a rueful smile. "No, it's not a gut idea to make up our minds out of fear."

"No, I guess not." Hannah stared at the rhubarb she held as if she'd forgotten what she was doing.

"We don't know what lies ahead, ain't so?" Mamm's voice was soft. "We just need to do the best we can."

Women's conversations, Hannah thought. Discussing everything over washing dishes or cleaning house or hanging up laundry. Talking about everything from simple household chores to raising children to faith and good works. Conversations that gave you strength and courage and sometimes even the conviction that you were doing right.

"One thing's certain," Hannah said. "We all want to protect our children—to keep them from making mistakes and to shield them and clear the path for them."

"We can't," her mother said firmly. "And if we could, we wouldn't like the results. We'd end up with children who think everything should come to them easily. They wouldn't know how to pick themselves up and try again."

"Yah, I guess you're right," she admitted. "But it seems so natural to protect them." She straightened up, realizing that her back ached and her bucket was filled. "There comes Annamae, and I still don't know what to say to her."

Mamm smiled at the frustration in her voice. "That's a sure sign you should leave it to God." She caught hold of Hannah by the shoulders so that they looked into each other's eyes. "The Lord will guide you. That's all you need to know."

Hannah held that thought close all the time she was greeting Annamae, showing her where to leave her horse and buggy, and returning to the rhubarb patch.

Her mother greeted Annamae with a welcoming smile. "We've got a good batch of rhubarb this year. We'll be glad to have you share some of it."

"My mother said to tell you how much we appreciate it. We've never had any success growing it, and she loves rhubarb sauce."

They worked in silence for a few minutes. Hannah knew she should say something, but what? This was her opportunity to help the girl if she could, but her mind was numb.

It was Annamae who broke the silence. "I heard that the bishop isn't well. I hope he's doing better now."

"My grandmother thinks he had too much sun," Hannah said.

"And too much worry," Mamm added firmly. "It's a big load the bishop carries."

Annamae froze with her hand on a stalk. When she looked up it was with tears in her eyes. "I heard my father say it was his fault. Then he shut up and didn't say anything more."

"It wasn't your responsibility, child," Mamm said quickly. "Your daad will have to settle that with Bishop Thomas himself." She stood up. "I'll go in and get the water boiling in the two big kettles. Why don't you two girls finish this row and then bring the rhubarb in?"

Her mother was giving her the opportunity to talk alone with Annamae, probably thinking Hannah hadn't done well so far.

She got Annamae's glance and smiled. "My mother is being tactful. Giving me a chance to talk to you alone."

"Yah. I thought maybe you wanted to." Annamae dropped her gaze.

"It's not easy being the youngest of the family, is it?" She kept her eyes on the girl's face, searching for any sign of a connection. "You and I have that in common."

Annamae blinked. "I guess we do." It was an opening, even if a small one.

"My sister says our parents fussed over me more than over all the older ones put together.

But she admits that she didn't want them fussing over her anyway."

"I didn't think about that, but I guess it's true enough. Why is that?"

Hannah shrugged. "They don't want their last baby to grow up, probably. I hope I'm not like that with my kids."

Annamae didn't seem interested in Hannah's parental struggles. Like most kids her age, she couldn't see further than her own problems. It was probably best to dive right in.

"Are things any better with your parents about you and Aaron?"

The girl shook her head. "Aaron is feeling so upset about it. He..." Annamae seemed about to say more, but she changed her mind.

"It was like that for me and Jonas, too," Hannah said, deliberately making the comparison.

"It was? But you got married here. I remember the wedding supper."

"Yah, we did, but only after a lot of struggle. My folks thought we were too young, but they finally agreed. It took longer to sway Jonas's father, Matthew, but he came around eventually."

"My daad would never—" Annamae began, but she let that trail off when she saw the twins running toward her from the daadihaus.

"Can we help?" Will reached for the knife, but Hannah caught his hand first.

"You can help us carry the rhubarb into the kitchen. I thought you were going to stay longer with your great-grandparents." She'd certain sure hoped they would.

"Bishop Thomas said he had to go and talk to someone," Elijah said. "And Grossmammi Nanny said he should rest."

"And he said—" Hannah cut off the rest of Will's comments by putting her hand across his lips.

"Enough. You shouldn't repeat what wasn't meant for you. Or listen, either."

"But Mammi..." Will spoke against her fingers, but a stern gaze stopped him. She thrust one of the pails into his hands.

"You two take that into the kitchen." Hannah let them get a little ahead of her and Annamae. "Sorry. Those two are little blabbermauls."

Annamae tried to smile, but it was obvious that she was disturbed. "It's about my daad, isn't it?"

"I don't know, and neither do you." She softened the curt note in her voice as best she could. She didn't want to antagonize the girl, but she didn't seem to be making much progress. "The bishop has a lot of other things to think about."

She set down the bucket she carried to put her arm around Annamae in a hug. She could hear her mother's voice saying something to the twins, but otherwise she and Annamae were as alone as they could be.

"I know things seem difficult right now. I remember how hard it was for Jonas and me."

"But you were able to get married. I don't think my daad will ever give in."

Hannah squeezed her, determined to find the way to reach the girl. "Aaron only sees one way out...to run away and get married. But is that really what you want? Do you think you're ready to be a wife and mother?"

Annamae hung her head for a moment. When she looked up, her tears were spilling over.

"There, now." Hannah pushed a tissue into her hand. "If you need to cry, it's okay."

It seemed that having permission to cry was enough to stop her tears. "I don't. But Aaron thinks it's the only thing to do. He says if I don't marry him, I'll break his heart, and he'll run away and never come back."

Hannah nodded, blinking back her own tears, and seeing Jonas clinging to her and hearing him saying almost the same words.

"I'll tell you a secret." She blotted Annamae's cheeks with a tissue. "Hearts don't break that easily. I thought mine would break when Jonas died, but my babies put it together again."

"But if he goes away, I'll never see him again," Annamae wailed.

It wouldn't do any good to tell her that she'd find someone else. Besides, Aaron was putting all the responsibility on her. She'd have to try a different track.

"Everyone thought we needed to grow up some more before getting married, but we got married anyway. And then we found we did have more growing up to do."

"But you and Jonas did, so it was all right," Annamae said, eager to have her idea upheld.

"I did, but Jonas didn't." Hannah was appalled at the words she heard coming from her lips. She didn't mean that, did she?

The words echoed in her heart. She knew the truth, even though she wanted to deny it. She had grown into being a mother, but Jonas had still been the boy he'd been the year they'd wed. Worse than that, she'd known it long before. Her instincts had told her they were too young, but she hadn't listened.

Annamae was staring at her, and the girl's lips formed a perfect *O*. Hannah took her arm and hustled her into the kitchen. There was nothing else she could say. Annamae's problems had led her into seeing what she'd never wanted to recognize, and now she'd have to learn to live with it.

Samuel closed the shop on the stroke of five. Bishop Thomas was hosting a supper for the chaperones of what people had begun to call the Matchmaking Project...not the bishop, however.

The bishop's goal was apparently to make the plans for the following weekend's visit. What Samuel wanted now was more personal. How had Hannah's talk with Annamae gone? The uncertainty hung on him like a weight.

If those two kids were going to create a scandal, he wanted to be far away when the explosion happened. How Hannah could remain so calm about it was beyond him. She didn't seem to understand that those kids risked messing up their whole future and leaving them to blame. He'd already been through that with Hannah and Jonas, and that was more than enough.

He'd be arriving at the farm in a few moments, so there ought to be time to catch Hannah alone. As he pulled up the lane, he scanned the backyard for a glimpse of Hannah, but she didn't seem to be there. The twins, though, were running toward him, and Samuel pulled up to avoid a collision.

"Whoa, take it easy."

Will scrambled up beside him while Elijah guided the horse to the hitching rail along the side of the barn. Only one buggy was there before him.

"You're early," Will exclaimed. "That's gut.

You can help get the hamburgers and hot dogs ready. I like hamburgers best."

"How about you, Elijah? What do you like best?"

"Hot dogs. So does Mammi because she says they're easy to make. What about you?"

"One of each," he said promptly. If they were going to argue, he wasn't taking sides. "Where's your mamm?"

"In the kitchen," Will said quickly. "You can go and help her. We'll show you." He grabbed one hand while Elijah took the other, and again he saw them exchange glances.

"You like our mamm, yah?" Elijah said gruffly.

"She likes you," Will said, as if answering a question.

Sam looked at them again as they went up the steps. What was going on now? Were they in trouble and looking for support?

"Gut. We all like each other." That seemed like a safe thing to say.

"Okay." Will nodded to his brother, and they both scooted off, leaving him shaking his head.

Hannah caught his gaze as he came into the kitchen and just as quickly looked away. Sam shook his head again. What was going on with everyone today?

He paused at the sink to greet Hannah's mother,

who was sorting silverware onto a tray. Her hands paused for a second.

"Samuel, it's gut you're here. Ready to help with the grilling?" Her smile, at least, was normal, and she glanced around the kitchen with the air of being in command. "Simon's already out there. And whatever you do, don't let Bishop Thomas help, or you'll be in trouble with Grossmammi."

"I'll do my best." He didn't want to be in trouble with either the bishop or his wife. He wasn't sure which would be worse.

Hannah had picked up a tray overloaded with hamburgers and hot dogs, and he took it from her. "Let me take that while you bring the grilling tools, yah?" he said.

"Denke." She managed to meet his gaze this time, smiling, but she still looked troubled.

Deciding to wait until they were out of earshot, Sam held the door open with his elbow until Hannah got through, and then he followed.

"You may as well tell me before we're surrounded again," he said. "Is it something about Annamae?"

Hannah seemed almost relieved. "I guess. We had time to talk while we put up what seemed like a thousand quarts of rhubarb sauce."

"That would give you time." His smile invited her to join in his appreciation.

"It did feel that way," she said, her lips curving.

"And what did you find out?" He almost hated to ask, knowing it would bring her worries back. "It's not any better?"

"No. At least I don't think so." Hannah glanced around as if making sure no one could hear. "It's Aaron. She says he's convinced that everyone is against them, and that the only way is to run away and get married." She set down the tray she carried. "And I could see she didn't want that."

He looked at her, not understanding. "That's good, ain't so? So long as she refuses to go away with him—"

"But will she?" Hannah snapped, looking as if she couldn't believe how dense he was. "He's putting pressure on her, making her feel she's the only thing keeping him from doing something foolish. Don't you see how hard that is for her? What if she gives in?"

In another moment Sam would have scoffed at that idea, but suddenly he realized they weren't just talking about Annamae and Aaron. They were talking about Hannah and Jonas, as well.

He put his hand over hers, ashamed he hadn't realized sooner. His first instinct was to blame the bishop for getting her into this to begin with, but that was worse than useless. It only took him round in a circle again. He knew, only too well, how intense the pressure was when you loved someone.

Sam wanted to ask a question, wanted to know what exactly Hannah thought about herself and Jonas. Was she saying that his pressure on Jonas had been too much? Or was it that Jonas's pressure on her to marry had been wrong?

As if feeling she'd revealed too much to him already, Hannah walked away quickly to consult with her father about the fire, leaving him alone and adrift.

Chapter Eleven

The next afternoon, Hannah pulled into the alleyway alongside the shop, heading for the hitching rail. The boys were ready to jump off the minute she stopped.

She had tried to explain that she was going there to help today, but the boys didn't seem able to picture what help she could be in the harness shop, so she let it go. Maybe stocking the shelves wasn't as exciting as running the sewing machine, but they'd learn it was necessary, too.

The big question in her mind was whether Samuel was willing and able to share any responsibility. He'd been running the shop with just Joseph to help since Matthew died, and even before that, Matthew's health problems had limited what he could do. His heart failure had grown worse, and it had seemed to Hannah that he had stopped fighting it.

Samuel had been faithful in coming to Matthew with decisions to be made, consulting him, trying to make him feel he was still a part of the shop, but it proved impossible to rouse him. She'd tried to interest him in the twins—after all, they were his grandsons, his link with Jonas. She still remembered her exasperation at his dismissive attitude toward them.

Should she have tried harder? Was there more that she could have done? She curbed her useless self-blame, and they drew up to the hitching rail.

The boys jumped down, engaged in their usual bickering over whose turn it was to tie the horse. It was a minor clash this time with her eyes on them, and they rushed ahead into the shop. She followed more slowly, carrying the basket that contained lunch.

The boys squealed with excitement when they entered to find Dorcas's oldest, Timothy, already there and helping Joseph cut a piece of leather. Timothy was one of their favorite people, and she just hoped the twins wouldn't distract him from the reason he was present.

Capturing them, she led them a safe distance and greeted Joseph and Samuel. "Now, don't pester Timothy. He's here to see if he could be an apprentice to Sam, learning about the business and helping."

"But we already do that," Will exclaimed. "We can do all those things."

The last thing she wanted was for the twins

to be jealous of Timothy, but before she could speak, Sam had interceded.

"Timothy is here to see if he likes leatherwork enough to want to learn it. Most boys and some girls do that after they leave school."

"And you're just starting school," Hannah reminded them. "You'll have to wait some time for that."

"Besides," Timothy added, "everyone knows you're going to be a partner in the business someday, even if you want to learn something else, too."

Hannah wasn't sure she appreciated having Timothy bring that up, but it was true. Maybe growing up with the idea in the back of their minds would be better for them.

"You probably have some work to do with Joseph and Timothy," she told Sam, veering the conversation in another direction. "If you'll show me what I should be working on, I'll get started." She waited for the response that would tell her whether he would let her share some store responsibility or not.

She could almost see the indecision on his face, but then he nodded. "Let's go up to the front, and I'll show you."

Well, it seemed that she had cracked the door open just a little, at least. They walked up to the counter together with the boys trailing along.

As usual, it didn't take long for Will to find something to say. "But isn't there something we can do?"

Hannah was about to suggest something helpful, as Mammi always did, but Sam beat her to it. "It's about time we opened. Do you want to do that?"

"Yah, sure." Will took a step toward the door, but Sam grasped his arm.

"Just a second until I tell you what that means. It means you'll clean the lower part of the windows, where people leave fingermarks, and then sweep the entrance to the shop. Cleaning tools are in the storeroom. Then you can unlock the door, put up the blinds and turn the door sign from Closed to Open. Got that?"

They raced each other back to the storeroom, and Hannah smiled at Sam. "You've learned the secret. Keeping them busy is the way to a good day."

"I'm beginning to see that. Should I keep you busy, as well?" His lips twitched.

"Definitely," she said, relaxing into a smile and feeling as if she'd achieved something. At least he was willing to let her help. Their unwilling partnership might turn out after all.

For a moment the two of them stood, looking at each other, and something that might have been affection moved between them. As if sensing that, Sam cleared his throat and turned toward a box he'd set on the floor.

"Here's a shipment of small items that came in last week." He picked it up and set it on the counter. "I haven't had time to deal with it." He sounded reluctant to admit it.

Hannah wanted to point out that he couldn't expect to do everything, but she felt uncertain about saying it and kept her peace.

"Just show me where you want it. Shall I keep a list?"

He seemed a little taken aback by her efficiency. "There should be an itemized list in the box. Just check them against that. I'll enter them in the books later."

She could see a way to make that process more efficient, but she could imagine Sam's reaction to her making changes already. He'd need some time to ease into the new situation, and she'd have to be tactful instead of charging ahead with her own ideas. Still, she couldn't help but feel a bit optimistic.

By this time, the twins had come back and begun the chores involved in opening the shop. One on either side of the door, they were cleaning the glass and making faces at each other through it. Smiling, Hannah found she was glancing around for Samuel. He'd gone back to working with Joseph, not paying attention to her or the twins.

Shrugging, she turned back to the boys. They seemed to be finished, so she rounded them up and set them to work on unpacking and sorting.

"You see, all of these horses' bits go in here." She pointed out the section of shelf that held one or two. "I'll count as we unpack, and you put them neatly in place."

For a time, the novelty kept them happy, but it began to wear off eventually. Will, as usual, was first to start fidgeting.

"I'm bored, Mammi. This isn't very important work." He filled the last bin on the bottom shelf.

"Not important?" She made the words sound unbelieving. "What would happen if a customer came in the door right now and asked to see the halter clips? What would you say?"

Elijah grinned. "I'd say, 'Right here.'"

"And Sam would be happy if we sold them, ain't so?" Will added. He glanced back at Sam, who was working on one of the machines.

"He's always nice to us," Elijah added. "So, it would be good to make him happy."

"We like him," Will said. "And he likes us."

That sounded like an echo of something they'd said before, and she gave them a second look. The older they got, the harder it was to tell what they were thinking. A glance into the probable future cost her a pang. What would happen when they were teenagers? How did a mother alone cope with that?

"You like him, don't you, Mammi?" Will was persistent. "It'd be gut to have a daadi, right, Elijah?"

Her stomach quivered. Their meaning popped into view very clearly. Matchmaking had been in the air, and the twins had picked it up. They were matchmaking. For some reason, they'd decided she needed a husband, so they'd picked one out.

Thoughts spinning, Hannah struggled to come up with an answer that would discourage them, or at least, slow them down.

"Yah, we all like each other." She chose her words carefully. "It's okay for you to want to have a daadi, but we have to wait for God to show us the right person."

To say nothing of the fact that both she and the potential husband had to feel it was right. Somehow, she didn't think she'd done enough to discourage them.

She'd always tried to give truthful answers to their questions, but some answers were complicated...too complicated to explain to a couple of five-year-olds.

Little though she wanted to bring it up with Samuel, maybe it would be best if she warned him about their ideas. Somehow doing that seemed even more complicated than explaining to the twins.

***

Samuel focused on the bridle he was making, running it through the machine a little more slowly than he usually would. Timothy stood at his elbow, watching intently, and Samuel saw his hands move as if he were guiding it.

Good, he told himself. The boy had the instinct to mimic Samuel's movements. Sam knew, from long practice, just what to do, but it would only become instinctive for Timothy through doing it again and again.

Having the apprentice at your elbow, watching, was the first step in the apprenticeship. He could remember how frustrated he'd been when Matthew started working with him and all he could do was watch. He'd wanted to jump onto the machine and try it out for himself.

He looked up, caught Timothy's glance and smiled. "It's good to watch how it's done a number of times before you try it yourself. You're teaching your hands and arms what to do."

Timothy nodded slowly. "I guess I see." He hesitated. "But I'd like to try it for myself." He said this last a little shyly, as if afraid to say the wrong thing.

"I know. That's what I thought myself when I started. Let's have a look at what you can do."

He was still standing at Timothy's side, watching the boy discover that it was a challenge to stitch a straight line in leather, when Hannah came by.

"I thought I'd make some coffee," she commented, smiling at the two of them. Or smiling only at the boy? Sam wasn't sure.

After a moment he followed Hannah to the back room, impelled by the feeling he'd forgotten to tell her something. He found her setting mugs on a tray while the coffeepot perked.

"Ready for a break?" she asked.

"Sounds good. There's some apple cider in the fridge if anybody wants it." He gestured to the small refrigerator he'd installed on a shelf in the corner. "I... I wondered how your grandfather is doing since his problem the other day."

"To hear him tell it, he's fine." A faint trace of worry showed in her eyes. "He's meeting with the ministers tonight, and they'll call on Annamae's father together." Her forehead wrinkled. "Please don't mention it to anyone."

Instinctively, he reached out and patted her arm. "No, of course not." He shook his head. "I'm glad the lot has never fallen on me. I wouldn't have the patience and kindness he shows."

"Ach, I know what you mean, but when one of my brothers said that, Grossdaadi told him that the gifts to do the job come from God when you offer yourself freely."

She glanced from his hand on her arm to his face, and he let go quickly. It had felt so natural that he hadn't even remembered doing it. Or maybe he hadn't chosen to remember.

"I'd best call the boys in for their drinks." He took a step toward the door, but this time it was Hannah who clasped his arm, stopping him. A flush mounted her face.

"I should tell you something." She seemed to have difficulty with the words. "The twins were talking just now, and I realized...well, I think they were trying to matchmake. Between us, I mean."

He started to say something, but she hurried on. "I tried to discourage them, but maybe they'll start hinting to you. So, I thought you should know ahead of time."

That needed thinking about, Sam decided. Was she saying that he should do the same and discourage them? Or was she apologizing in advance if the idea upset him?

Surprisingly, it didn't upset him at all, but he didn't understand why. He found the twins interesting, and he'd never yet been upset in the least by their questions.

Maybe that wasn't the right thing to say. He wouldn't want her to think he was interfering in her life. He'd already done that, with difficult results.

He spoke slowly, considering each word. "I... I don't know if they'll say anything to me, but if they do...well, do you want me to discourage them? Whatever you say about the boys goes."

Hannah turned away, picking up her mug. "Yah, that would be good. I'll send them back for their cider."

She went out quickly, leaving Sam to consider whether he'd said the right thing or not. He could hear her footsteps retreating as she called the boys to have something to drink.

The door clattered open, its bell jangling, and he went to the door to see who had come in so noisily.

"Katie!" Hannah exclaimed. "What's wrong?"

Katie hurried to Hannah, her face distraught. "I need to talk to you and Samuel. It's Annamae. She sent me. She told me to hurry."

Hannah was thankful that no customers were in the shop as she put her arm around Katie's waist, trying to soothe the girl. "It's all right." She beckoned to Samuel. "We're both here. Calm down now."

Seeing the twins looking on with wide eyes, she spoke to them quietly. "You two go in the back room. There's some apple cider for a snack, and I put a tin of cookies there, too."

When they hesitated, reluctant to leave what

appeared to be a scene of excitement, she frowned. "Now," she said firmly. It was the tone that usually got results, and Will grabbed his brother's hand and tugged him toward the back room.

"Hurry," Katie said, clutching her arm. "You have to do something."

"First you have to calm down and tell us quietly what's wrong. Take a deep breath, then another one." Her gaze met Samuel's, and it steadied her. Whatever was wrong, she wasn't in it alone.

Katie took another long breath, and Hannah could feel her relaxing. Katie pressed her lips together and then nodded.

"Yah, okay. Sorry." Katie's voice had steadied, and she sucked in another breath. "Annamae hurried over to our place just a little bit ago. She said that Aaron was going to run away and wanted her to go with him."

Hannah wasn't really that surprised, she realized. "What is Annamae going to do?"

Katie's bright blue eyes dazzled with tears. "She said to tell you. To say that she'd keep trying to convince him to turn back, but she couldn't let him go alone."

Samuel made an impatient sound. "Where? Do you know where they were headed? Think, Katie."

She nodded. "Annamae said to tell you probably Lewisburg. Aunt Dorcas tried to get her to stay with us, but she wouldn't. She just ran out and got in the buggy. Then Aunt Dorcas said to come for you as fast as I could. She said I should bring the boys home with me so Joseph could mind the shop. She said she knows you and Samuel will go after them."

Hannah realized she didn't even have to look at Samuel to know he'd be with her. With a quick nod, he headed out the back to bring the buggy around.

"Good job," she said, squeezing Katie. "Just tell everyone not to talk about it, all right? And pray we get them back fast enough so there's not a big fuss."

Surprisingly enough, there wasn't even a small fuss. Katie supervised the boys' snacks while she talked to her cousin Timothy. Then Timothy said it would be best if he stayed with Joseph, and Hannah, stressing the importance of not talking about it, hurried out the front door just as Samuel brought the buggy around.

In another moment she had clasped Samuel's hand while he swung her up to the seat, and they were off.

Hannah's hands were shaking, and she clasped them together in her lap. She couldn't let herself fall apart now. This was the time for action. Later she'd be able to spend all the time she wanted feeling guilty and thinking she should have done something different, but not now.

Chapter Twelve

They were finally clear of town, and Samuel slowed the buggy as they approached Pine Hollow Road. "What do you think? Would they stay on the main road, or would they take the back roads?" Samuel was looking at Hannah as if he expected an answer.

Her thoughts spinning wildly, Hannah tried to focus on Annamae and Aaron. "How can I guess which way they'd go?"

Samuel drew to the side of the road. "Just stop. Take a deep breath, like you told Katie."

Hands shaking again, she clasped them tighter. "I can't... I can't."

She expected a curt order telling her not to be foolish, but instead she felt Samuel's warm, strong hand enveloping hers. "Steady. Relax. Breathe."

He was doing what she had done with Katie, and she felt it begin to work. Reassurance flowed through his touch, warming and calming her.

"That's the way," he said quietly. "Empty your

mind and listen to your instincts. What do they tell you?"

Hannah blinked, shooting a glance at him. "You're telling me to rely on my instincts?"

The corners of his mouth twitched. "I know I've never thought much of them, but I've seen them work fairly well in the past few weeks. What are they telling you now?"

Thinking about the many twists and turns of the farm lanes that led toward the larger town, where the runaways could catch a bus to almost anywhere, she compared it with the main road with its heavier vehicle traffic. Which?

"The back roads," she said, not stopping to think further. Doubts assailed her almost immediately. What if she was wrong?

Samuel must have felt her own doubts. "Sure?"

"Yes." Saying the word made her sure. "They wouldn't have much experience of driving on the main roads. They'd stick to the familiar. Besides, Annamae wants time to convince Aaron this is the wrong choice."

"Okay." He flicked the reins. "I just wanted to be sure you were listening to your own impressions of them."

She eyed him curiously as they started down Pine Hollow Road. "That sounds unusual for you. I thought you just relied on your view of right and wrong."

"Yah, I do. But the right thing is clear in this case. We have to find them before we can do anything. You know both of those youngsters better than I do, so I'll follow your instincts."

He fell silent, working his way cautiously around a wagon whose driver was taking up more than his share of the road. Once clear, he picked up speed again.

Finding she had nothing to do but relax and let him drive, Hannah leaned against the back of the seat. She watched Sam's strong, steady hands on the lines. He wouldn't be sending any contradictory messages through his touch to the horse.

They passed a large field of corn, already close to knee-high, and beyond it rows of soybeans reaching toward the sun. The farms along the road alternated between Amish and Englisch.

A rickety sign invited passersby to pick their own strawberries, and behind it healthy-looking plants were abundant with berries turning red. Their own strawberries would be ready in another day or two, announcing a busy time of picking and jam-making.

Samuel's expression was as steady as his hands. It was rare to read his thoughts through his expression, because he wasn't a man who showed much. In comparison, Jonas's lively face had shown every fleeting, volatile thought.

Sam startled her with a quick glance, which

again said that he knew what she had been thinking. "Well? Have you decided to trust me?"

"There was never any doubt of it," she said, not wanting to disturb her inner confidence. "I've always known you would do exactly what you think is right. And in this case, we're both sure of what that is." She hesitated, again reluctant to shatter the peace between them. "Are you still wishing we'd never gotten involved with Annamae and her problems?"

His shoulders moved in a slight shrug. "I can think of better ways to be spending the day."

"My grandfather always says that if God puts someone in need right in front of you, it means that person is your job."

"I know. It's one of his favorite sermons, yah? I'd say that's right. But I can see an ugly scene with Annamae's father coming up in front of us, too."

She nodded, feeling sure he was right, but also sure they'd face it together. Samuel would probably still say they should have told Annamae's parents to begin with. But she'd at least convinced him to talk it over with the bishop.

Samuel nudged her. "You're worrying again. Stop it. We'll find them."

"Yah." She rubbed her fingers across her forehead. "If only Aaron had had a little more patience. He reminds me of..." She stopped, seeing where that sentence was taking her.

"He reminds you of Jonas, ain't so?" Samuel's voice was even, but she thought he worked to keep it that way. Would Jonas always stand between them?

She took her time about answering, but given how far they'd come in recent weeks, she knew she had to.

"The situation reminds me of Jonas," she said. "But I don't know Aaron well enough to say whether he is like Jonas. For sure he's feeling that everyone is against them, like Jonas did, but really, it seems that Annamae's father is the cause of the problems."

He shook his head, and she sensed the movement even though she wasn't looking at him. "Jonas's father was trying to do what he thought was right, I'm sure of that. And I hope you've stopped thinking that Matthew was opposed to the wedding because he didn't like you. Matthew—"

"It doesn't matter," she interrupted quickly. "I have forgiven and forgotten whatever I believed at the time. It's probably true that we were too immature for marriage. Or at least that Jonas was."

She held her breath, wondering if he would spring to Jonas's defense. She'd said what she believed to be true, and she couldn't do other than that.

"Look!" Samuel pointed ahead of them to

where the narrow road made a sharp turn to the right.

An Amish buggy was tilted on its side, its right-side wheels sinking into a small, muddy stream. Annamae and Aaron were trying to get out, and even as they watched, Annamae slid knee-deep in the creek.

Samuel felt a mix of emotions as he drew up behind the tip-tilted buggy. Relief that they'd found the pair of runaways was submerged by exasperation at their predicament and the wish that Annamae's father was here to take care of his own problem.

Jumping down, he was aware of Hannah sliding down behind him. He reached the girl, who was struggling for footing, grabbed her by the waist and swung her out onto the dry surface of the road. Aaron was struggling as well, but the boy was embarrassed enough already. Needing help to get out would just make things worse.

As soon as her feet touched the road, Annamae rushed to Hannah and flung herself into her welcoming arms. Sam couldn't help it...his lips twitched. So Aaron and Annamae thought they were old enough to be married? They couldn't even cope with driving down a country lane.

He turned to Aaron, and despite his exasperation, he couldn't help feeling sorry for the boy.

Wet and splashed with mud, he couldn't bring himself to meet Samuel's eyes. What was he going to do when faced with Annamae's father? Or his own? Or the bishop?

Shaking his head, he moved closer to the buggy, hoping this part of the trouble would be easy to solve. If he took care of the buggy and the boy, Hannah could cope with the rest of the situation. He had no idea what would come next.

Aaron sloshed his way out of the stream and moved to his horse's head. Samuel had to approve—at least Aaron knew he had to take care of his animal. Aaron soothed the gelding, running his hands down the near legs cautiously.

"Seems all right," he muttered, still flushed and embarrassed.

"Good," Sam said briskly. "Check the far side, and then we'll see about getting the buggy out."

Aaron looked relieved, apparently realizing Samuel wasn't going to berate him—or at least, not yet. "Yah. Denke."

Patting the gelding's flank, Sam checked the harness, realizing it was one of his and glad to see it was in good shape. No problems with the buggy itself that he could see. It appeared that Aaron had just steered it off the road.

He guessed that Hannah expected him to talk to the kid, whether he wanted to or not.

"So how did you get into this predicament, anyway?"

Shamefaced, Aaron looked up. "Guess I wasn't paying enough attention."

As peacefully as he could, Samuel went on, "You were talking to Annamae?"

Aaron nodded. "Yah. Arguing, more like. Annamae said...something, and when I looked, there was a pickup coming in the middle of the road. I tried to get over, and the back wheels started to slide."

"It happens." He hesitated a moment, but he might as well try to get a little more out of Aaron. "What did Annamae say that made you not notice a pickup?"

Aaron's flushed bright red. "She said she wouldn't marry me. She said we weren't old enough."

Sam resisted the impulse to point out that current circumstances seemed to prove that.

"I guess every man faces something like that once in a while. Takes time to find the right woman." It certain sure had taken him a long time. And even if he had, he doubted that Hannah would agree.

"Yah." Aaron looked a little better for having been talked to man to man. "Then I saw the pickup, and—"

"You ended up in the ditch and felt even worse."

"Guess I did." Aaron managed a slight smile. "Suppose you get in back and push, and I'll take the head. That's a problem we can solve, ain't so?"

After a few minutes of straining and slipping, there was a loud splash and the buggy moved. After that, it only took a matter of minutes to get the buggy back on the road. The horse, relieved to have solid ground beneath his hooves, shook his head, setting the harness jingling.

Aaron took hold of the animal's head and looked uncertainly at Samuel. "What now?"

Samuel shrugged. "I guess that's up to you. I'm not your daad, but if I were, I'd say that no problem is made better by running away."

The boy's expression didn't change for a moment, but then he broke into a smile. "Yah, I guess. I'd best go home. Will Annamae…?"

"We'll take her home. Go say your goodbyes." Ground-tying the horse, they walked together to where Hannah stood with her hand on Annamae's arm.

Aaron came to a halt. Flushing, he managed to get some words out. "Sorry, everybody. Annamae, do you want me to go with you to face your father?"

"No." Her voice was shrill at the thought. "I'll be okay."

Aaron nodded awkwardly, then walked quickly

back to the buggy. Sam turned back to find Hannah shepherding the girl into the back seat before climbing into the front. He swung up beside her. "What now?" he queried.

Hannah studied his face and seemed to relax, her lips curving. "Let's go back to our place. Grossdaadi will help to handle it."

She sounded sure of herself, and he nodded, picking up the lines. The situation had been a mess, but he had the feeling that it was clearing up for the best.

Thanks to Hannah, he had to admit.

As they neared the farm lane, Hannah scrutinized Samuel's face. He'd said very little during the drive, while she kept turning her face to talk reassuringly to Annamae in the back seat. Was he just silent because he wanted her to talk to the girl? Or was he dreading the scene to come with the bishop and Annamae's father?

His firm jaw and the lines between his straight eyebrows didn't tell her anything, and her heart sank. In recent days she'd sometimes thought she knew what Samuel was thinking, but now she didn't have a clue.

She and Grossdaadi had gotten him into this situation, that was certain sure. But she had confidence that her grandfather would find a way to make this come right.

Should she begin by pointing out the girl had just gone with Aaron to convince him not to run away, or should she leave Annamae to speak for herself? Another glance at Samuel's face didn't provide her with an answer, and they were pulling up to the kitchen door.

Samuel turned to her, seeming about to speak, but her mother came hurrying out to wrap Annamae in a big hug. "Ach, you're here and safe. Komm, we'll go in and get some food into you. A bowl of beef vegetable soup and some hot tea will make you feel better."

Mammi glanced back at Hannah and Sam as she hustled the girl up the back steps. "And you two, as well. We have some supper staying warm. Komm along."

Hannah had to suppress a smile. She wasn't laughing at her mother, just thinking how predictable she was. Hugs and hot food were her immediate answer to trouble. Sam might have used the opportunity to escape, but he didn't. Instead, he touched her arm reassuringly as they followed along into the kitchen.

Getting them seated, Mamm started dipping up steaming bowls of soup, acting as if all of them had been in the creek instead of the buggy.

"The bishop will be along soon," she added, setting a bowl of soup in front of Annamae and adding a basket of crusty bread to the table.

"Now you just get outside of that, and you'll feel better."

Annamae gave her a cautious look. "Do my parents know I'm all right?"

"Yah, for sure." Mammi patted the girl's shoulder. "The bishop and the ministers talked with your daad earlier."

Annamae looked as if that news was not exactly reassuring, but she spooned up some soup. After a few spoonfuls, her color started to come back, and Hannah relaxed a little. One thing about girls her age...they had resilience. Annamae should be none the worse for this experience so long as her parents handled it wisely.

Before she could consider the likelihood of that, her grandfather was coming into the kitchen from the grossdaadi haus, and almost at once she heard the sound of another buggy.

Grossdaadi patted Annamae on the shoulder. "That will be your parents. Be patient with them."

Annamae's eyes widened. Apparently, that was the last advice she'd thought to receive from the bishop. She stood up slowly, stepping away from the table as her parents came in.

To Hannah's surprise, Annamae's father was the first to reach her. He drew her into a hug, his expression struggling with emotion. Then her mother was there, as well, and the three of them held on to each other tightly, murmuring softly and wiping away tears.

Whatever the bishop and the ministers had said, it had taken root in Ephraim's heart. His red eyes said he'd been crying. Tears clouded Hannah's own vision, so that she saw the family through a haze of light and shadow. Glancing at her grandfather, she saw that his head was bent in prayer.

A light touch on her arm drew her attention to Samuel. If he'd been affected by the result for Annamae, he wasn't showing it. For a moment she was exasperated, but she reminded herself that Samuel wasn't one to show his emotions on his face.

Samuel gestured toward the door. Perhaps he thought the two of them weren't necessary just now. He was right, she decided. For sure she didn't want to discuss the situation with Annamae's father. It would be so easy to say the wrong thing and undo the good Grossdaadi had done.

She nodded in agreement, and the two of them slipped toward the door. Samuel's hand closed around hers as if to be sure she didn't go anywhere else.

When they'd reached the buggy without anyone calling them back, she heard Samuel give a sigh of relief.

"Thank the good Lord I've never been called

to be a minister. I have enough trouble deciding what is right for me, and I still make mistakes."

He looked so rueful that Hannah had to smile. "Grossdaadi has lived much longer than either of us. He's had time to gather a lot of wisdom."

"Yah."

Samuel patted the gelding on the shoulder and unclasped the line keeping the horse at the hitching rail. She felt a little let down. Was that all he had to say? Maybe the reminder of her decision about Jonas hadn't affected him as it had done her.

Or if he did think about it, maybe he was just relieved to leave all that in the past. Sam glanced down, seeming to realize that he was still holding her hand. She could almost feel the warmth and strength of him flowing into her, tingling along her nerves straight to her heart.

Hannah's gaze flew to his face. She tried to find something to say that would ease the moment, but nothing at all came to her mind. It was as if they were stalled there, each aware of the other, neither knowing what to do.

So quickly that she didn't see it coming, he bent and kissed her. His lips were warm on hers, and she could feel herself responding.

But then, before she could say a word, he swung himself up to the buggy seat and was gone.

Chapter Thirteen

By the time Hannah was getting the boys ready for bed, she was ready for any distraction, even if it meant chasing down the dirty clothes that had missed the laundry basket. Normally she would have waited while the twins did it themselves, but right now it kept her from thinking of Samuel and trying to figure out what that kiss had meant.

"Sorry, Mammi." Will scrambled around the basket to pick up a sock that had become lost from its mate.

"It's all right. You'll do better next time." For a moment he looked as if he speculated about the possibility of that happening.

Elijah nudged him. "Ask her," he said.

Will frowned and rubbed his arm. "Go ahead. You do it."

"You said you would." Elijah carried on with their usual back-and-forth. They'd probably be doing the same when they were in their forties.

"Whatever it is, somebody ask me." Her voice

was sharper than she intended, and she softened it with a smile.

It was Elijah who spoke up. "Will thought... well, we both thought...that Sam would stay around tonight so we could see him. We wondered why he didn't. We wanted to talk to him."

She felt exactly the same, but she couldn't say so. "Maybe he had work to do. We'll probably see him in the next day or two. Komm, now. On your knees for prayers."

"Can we ask God to make Sam come back tomorrow?" They started to slide down, but Will wasn't satisfied. "Grossdaadi says if two people agree in what they're asking, God will give it to them."

Hannah's head had started to throb, and she wondered why they came up with the most complicated questions at bedtime.

"I don't think you have that exactly right," she said, pointing to the spot beside each bed where they knelt for prayers. "Besides, you wouldn't want Sam to come if he had something else important to do."

"Yah, we would," they echoed in chorus.

Chuckling in spite of herself, she rested a hand on each small head. Not so small, though. She remembered when each twin's head was the size of an orange...when they were so tiny there was a question whether they could ever catch up in size.

But they did. Now they were both strong and healthy, their hair curling around her fingers no matter how hard they tried to flatten it.

"That wouldn't be the action of a friend, to make him miss something important. And Sam is your friend, isn't he?"

Something squeezed her heart. Sam was her friend, wasn't he? She'd thought so. But maybe that kiss meant he wanted something more. Her heart thudded rapidly.

Trying to ignore it, she spoke as calmly as she could. "Suppose you tell God you want to see Sam and let Him decide when it's the best time. Now, get on with your prayers."

Fortunately, the twins still recognized the voice that meant Mammi was done arguing. They clasped their hands and lowered their faces until their fingertips touched their chins. As always, their prayers consisted of each one taking a turn to pray before asking God to bless all of their loved ones. She noticed they included Sam in that list.

Please, Lord, don't let them be hurt, she murmured silently.

She bent over each small bed for kisses and tucked their quilts snugly around them. The quilts might be on the floor by morning, but each night had to begin this way.

"Sleep well," she whispered, turning off the lamp on the table between the beds. "God bless."

Hannah slipped out into the hall quietly, relieved when she reached it without any interruption. A few steps took her to the top of the stairs, where she slid down to sit on the top one, feeling as if her legs wouldn't hold her up any longer.

What a day it has been, she told herself, feeling the tiredness seep through her. All that worry about Annamae had just been the start. She leaned her forehead against her arm. At least that had seemed to turn out well. Her grandfather had said that Ephraim had responded positively to their visit, and when the news came that Annamae was gone, he hadn't hesitated to blame himself. Whether that would last or not, at least it was good for the moment.

A month ago she had been settled in a life that suited her, taking care of her sons, surrounded by family, satisfied to have life go on as it was. Then Grossdaadi had asked her to help with the matchmaking project, and everything slid out of control.

And then today, and that kiss from Samuel...

The boys wanted to know why Sam had left so quickly. So did she, didn't she?

Samuel was alone in the shop, trying to catch up on a backload of orders and doing his best to concentrate. He had always found this the most satisfying way of working. Get at it early in the morning, before Joseph arrived, before shoppers were coming in and out and distracting him.

He hadn't slept well, and it had been a relief to finally see the eastern sky lightening, reflecting from the clouds and giving Sam a good reason to stop tossing and turning and get up. Deciding he'd eat breakfast later, he sat down at his favorite sewing machine, put other thoughts out of his mind and concentrated on the stitching for a new harness.

The leather moved smoothly through the machine with a minimal amount of guidance on his part, and his pulses slowed. He could feel himself getting into the rhythm of the work, his mind moving ahead of the machine as his muscles relaxed. There was no reason to let himself get tense. All he had to do was to leave the past behind, focusing on the work in his hands.

Samuel sank himself into the work, not surfacing until he heard the rattle of the side door. It would be Joseph, since no one else had a key to that door, and Timothy was right behind him. The boy was enthusiastic, even Joseph had to admit that. He was on time or early every day he was scheduled to work.

Joseph always came in as noisily as one man could, and with the boy along that was very noisy indeed. Joseph was an early bird, chattering busily like the swallows in the stable behind the building. If Samuel didn't respond, he'd talk to himself, and answer himself, as well. That would grow so annoying that Sam had to talk in self-defense.

"Looks like rain coming on," he said, stopping by the back room to hang up the lightweight jacket he wore every day, sunny or not. "Probably not a lot of customers coming in."

"It'll give us a chance to get caught up on some of these orders," Sam said, nodding to Timothy. "This harness for Delbert Marsh is almost finished." He stood, stretching, and realized he hadn't thought about Hannah for at least an hour.

"Nice." Joseph came over to have a look. "We were plenty busy when you were out yesterday. I made a note of some things that need to be restocked."

"Good."

Sam was surprised. Joseph didn't usually like to be bothered by things like that, focusing instead on the sewing.

Joseph grinned. "I guess actually I told the boy to do it. He writes better than I do. Adds better, too. Comes of not being away from school very long."

Timothy just smiled, accepting that explanation whether he believed it or not.

For sure, any kind of paperwork was foreign to Joseph's thinking, and Sam suspected he hadn't been much different even when he was in school himself.

"Your favorite Englisch horsewoman was here yesterday, too. Disappointed not to see you."

"If you mean Ms. Chapel, call her by name. Customers don't like it if you don't remember their names. And she's not my favorite, even if she's yours."

"Doesn't explain why she always wants to talk to you," Joseph said. "Maybe you ought to get married. That would keep other women away, yah?"

A flicker of annoyance disrupted his thoughts. Whenever Joseph wanted to get his goat, he'd bring up the idea of getting married.

"Not interested," he said, hoping to cut him off.

"Not even in a pretty Amish widow? Somebody sweet and kind, maybe with a couple of kids who need a father?"

"You must be talking about yourself," he retorted. "Alice has been gone a good ten years. Time for you to remarry."

Joseph sobered at once, and Sam felt guilty. He knew better than to bring up Joseph's deeply mourned wife. He'd been desperate to stop Joseph from teasing him about Hannah.

"Nobody could take Alice's place."

Feeling guilty, Sam put his hand on Joseph's shoulder for a moment in silent apology. They knew each other so well it didn't take anything else.

"Guess I'll make some coffee," he said, and went on into the back room.

He'd already made up his mind that he needed to step back from Hannah and the twins. He'd had a satisfying life before he'd started seeing so much of her in the past month. He couldn't stop seeing them entirely—he had obligations to them.

Standing at the sink, he began filling the coffeepot, but his thoughts still churned. Maybe he could ease himself out of the matchmaking project. That would cut down on the time they spent together.

It made sense to do so. He had plenty of work on hand to occupy him. And Hannah didn't need him around reminding her of his opposition to her marriage to Jonas.

He might not understand women very well, but that he did know. So why in the world had he lost control and kissed her?

The image wasn't far from his conscious thoughts, and he saw it again. Hannah's heart-shaped face lifted to his, her eyes dark and wondering...he'd looked, he'd touched and he'd fallen. Next thing he'd known he had his arms around her and was touching her soft lips with his.

Running away was the worst thing he could have done. He should have stepped back, apologized at once and promised it would never happen again. Then maybe they could have gone back to where they'd been before.

The splash of cold water on his sleeve brought him back to the present with a shock. He shut off the faucet and mopped himself with a dish towel. Frowning, he started the coffee, standing at the counter waiting for it.

Someone rang the doorbell on the shop door, apparently not willing to wait until they'd opened. He heard Joseph go to the door, heard the murmur of voices and then the door closed again. Joseph had handled it, whatever it was.

A few minutes later, carrying the two mugs of coffee, he went out to join Joseph. As he set one down, Joseph held out a half sheet of paper.

"Message for you. The bishop wants you to come for supper tonight." Joseph lifted his eyebrows. "Have you been getting into trouble?"

It took an effort to deny it, considering how guilty he felt. Maybe he wouldn't have to pull out of the matchmaking project himself. Maybe the bishop would do it for him. That might be the best solution.

* * *

Hannah stepped outside to call the twins in for supper. There was no answer. She shouted again, a bit louder, hoping they hadn't gone out of earshot. She wanted to get back to the kitchen before her grandmother tried to lift something too heavy for her. With Mamm and Daad over at Mamm's sister's for the evening, the responsibility rested on her.

"Boys!" she shouted again and finally heard an answer from the barn. "Come to supper." They appeared in the wide barn door, waving, and started to run toward her.

Hurrying back inside, she was just in time to catch her grandmother trying to lift the heavy roasting pan from the oven.

"Wait a sec. I'll get it." She hurried to her grandmother's side.

"I can do it," Grossmammi said tartly, offended at the suggestion that there was something in the kitchen she couldn't do.

"For sure you can," Hannah said, grabbing the handles with potholders. "But I'm right here." Together they lifted it onto the stovetop.

"Let the child help," Grossdaadi said, winking at Hannah. "You taught her everything she knows."

"That's true." Hannah bent to kiss Grossmammi's soft, crinkled cheek. Someday she'd probably be just as sensitive about any hint that she couldn't do what she once had.

The twins burst through the back door. "We're here," Will announced. "Is supper ready?"

"It will be by the time you've washed up," Grossdaadi told him, grabbing Will's hand before he could touch the table. "Off you go."

"And use soap," Hannah added. "Don't just wipe the dirt off on the towel."

They raced each other back to the sink in the mudroom, jostling each other in the doorway as Hannah and her grandmother served the hot dishes onto the table. Once they were back, everyone was ready for the blessing.

"What were you doing in the barn?" she asked as the food went around. "You must have been busy to keep you from hearing me."

"Yah, we were—" Elijah's answer was cut off abruptly, and Hannah suspected his brother had kicked him.

"We made up a new game," Will said quickly.

Before she had time to inquire further, her grandfather was leaning back to peer out the window. "Ach, I forgot," he exclaimed. "There is Samuel. I asked him for supper. I want to talk to him about everything that happened with Annamae."

Her grandmother started to rise, used to the bishop inviting people to a meal without telling her.

"I'll get it, Grossmammi." Hannah scrambled to her feet, eager to be busy while Samuel was coming in and being welcomed warmly by her grandparents and noisily by the twins.

Like her grandmother, she was used to unexpected guests, but the sight of Samuel brought all of her scattered emotions surging to the forefront of her mind. She had to concentrate to keep her hands steady as she lifted down another table setting. If only she'd known…but what good would it have done? She could think about it all day without coming up with a good explanation for that kiss.

By this time talk was bouncing around the table, and she was content to let it flow. The next move was up to Samuel, she told herself. He was the one who'd run away.

She glanced at him, noting the tight line of his jaw and the way he avoided looking at her. It seemed as if he was having just as much trouble with this encounter as she was. Somehow that made her feel better.

Talk bounced around the table as it always did once they started eating. As usual, the boys didn't chip in until they'd eaten their first helpings. Then they talked nonstop while their great-grandfather teased them about how much they talked.

By the time she'd served the coffee and pie,

Grossdaadi and Samuel vanished into the daadi haus, and the boys hurried outside to do their evening chores. It took some doing, but she finally managed to convince her grandmother to sit down with her quilt patches in the front room, leaving Hannah to finish the dishes.

Adding hot water and some additional detergent, Hannah tackled the pots and pans, all the while listening for someone coming out of the daadihaus. She couldn't imagine what Grossdaadi was telling Samuel other than what he'd already said to her...that they had handled the situation well, that Annamae's father had been frightened enough by learning that his daughter had disappeared to have learned a valuable lesson.

For a moment, she found herself thinking about her own boys. What would it be like when they were rumspringa age? Would she have the wisdom to handle two teenagers, especially without a spouse?

She was focused so intently upon that issue that she almost missed the sound of Samuel coming back to the kitchen. She spun around at the sound of his step, dropping the spatula she'd been washing so that it clinked onto the floor.

She bent to pick it up and came close to cracking heads with Samuel. They each made a grab for the spatula and stood up with their hands entangled, soap bubbles dripping from them.

"Ach, you'll get all wet. Let me..." she began. The words trailed away as she saw Sam's gaze intent on her face.

"It won't hurt me to be a little wet," he said softly, still focusing on her face. "I deserve worse than that."

"Worse?" she murmured, feeling the room spin around them, drawing them closer together.

"Yah, worse." His fingers wrapped around her wrist, and she found she was wondering if he could feel the rapid thudding of her pulse. "After all, I'm the one who kissed you and ran away."

It was what she'd been thinking herself, but it seemed suddenly trivial. Why then couldn't she find anything to say?

"It...it doesn't matter," she said, stumbling over the words.

"Of course it matters." His fingers tightened on her wrist. "Do you think I would kiss you if it didn't matter to me? We're both too old for casual kissing, ain't so?"

She wasn't sure she wanted to admit that. "What did it mean?" she managed to ask.

"It meant I had feelings for you. Feelings I didn't even know I had." He lifted the hand he held captive to his lips, his breath moving across her skin. "Do you feel the same?"

"I don't know." She couldn't find another answer. She had forgiven him. She had worked with him, laughed with him, enjoyed his presence, even shared her sons with him, but…

"It's all right." The words brushed against her fingers. "You need time. It's not just the two of us, ain't so? You have to think about the boys, too." He dropped a kiss on her hand and brushed her cheek lightly with his fingertips. "I can wait. Just…don't make it too long."

Predictably, the boys' footsteps pounded up the steps onto the porch at that instant. She looked up and saw the laughter in his eyes, and she smiled. It felt as if the connection between them was so strong that it didn't need words. That should surprise her, but instead it felt exactly right.

Chapter Fourteen

Hannah drifted through what remained of the day, and her dreams that night must have been happy ones, because she woke up smiling. She tried to contain herself as she dressed and got ready for the day. Nothing had been decided yet. As Samuel had said, it wasn't just a matter of a young couple joining their lives together. The twins were an important consideration.

True, they seemed to like Samuel, but were they ready to have him for a father? And was he ready to be a father to them? He hadn't had much experience with children as far as she knew. He'd been like an older brother to Jonas, but that hadn't ended well.

That thought was enough to obscure the visions that had floated through her dreams. She reminded herself that she had forgiven him for his part in that unhappy time. He'd been caught between his commitment to his mentor and his friendship with Jonas, she could see that now.

She heard the twins clattering down the stairs

and roused herself to follow them. She should be getting breakfast ready—she'd overslept, and no one had called her.

Hurrying down the stairs, she found her mother cooking a pan of scrapple with one hand and stirring scrambled eggs with the other.

"Ach, Mammi, I'm sorry." She took the spatula in her own hand and slid it under the crisp edges of a slice of the meat mixture. "I should have been down earlier. Why didn't you call me?"

Her mother laughed. "This is nothing compared to what it was like when your brothers and sisters were home. Besides, I wouldn't want to disrupt any sweet dreams."

Hannah shot her a quick glance, but her mother didn't show any awareness that Hannah's dreams might have been unusual. She couldn't know what had happened last night, Hannah assured herself.

The boys were setting the table, making their usual amount of clatter about it. Will dropped a handful of forks on the table so that they bounced off a plate.

"If you break anything…" she began.

"I didn't, Mammi." He gave the plate a careless glance. "Mammi, Joey Mueller says that the girls set the table at their house. He says that it's not a boy's job."

"If Joey Mueller lived here, he'd find it was his job," she responded.

"You see any girls around?" Grossmammi entered the kitchen in time to hear that exchange. "If you find any, they can help you."

That was enough to silence Will, and he managed to finish setting the table without more noise. She repressed a smile. Grossmammi still knew how to cope with a sassy little boy.

Mammi glanced toward the window and began scooping scrambled eggs into a bowl. "The men are coming. Is that scrapple about ready?"

"Just getting it up now." Hannah forked crisp pieces onto a platter.

"Mammi, are we going to the harness shop today?" Elijah was looking at her questioningly, blue eyes hopeful.

"Yah, after you've finished your morning chores." She could feel warmth rising in her cheeks at the thought and ducked her head, hoping no one had noticed.

Daad and Grossdaadi came in from the mudroom, a little wet from vigorously washing their hands after milking.

"If you're going into town, you'd best go early," Daad said, glancing out the window at the sky. "It looks like a storm coming."

Hannah glanced out at the clouds gathering above the ridge to the west. "Yah, we'll go soon."

Daadi was looking at her curiously, as if about to say something else, but Mammi got in first. "Better throw the boys' jackets in, just in case."

It sounded as if everyone wanted to see her leave. She thought of Samuel and suppressed the desire to agree with them. Yah, she wanted to see him, but she didn't care to have everyone else know how she felt.

She caught her mother's gaze and suspected that it was too late for that. But how could her mother know anything about her feelings for Samuel? She and Daad hadn't returned until well after Sam had left. She must be imagining things.

Mammi and Grossmammi seemed in a rush to get everyone out the door as quickly as possible today. Before they knew what was going on, the boys had been rushed out to finish their chores, with the men right behind them.

"At last," her mother said. "I thought they'd never go."

"What are you talking about?" Hannah planted her hands on her hips. "You've been hustling everyone along since we got up."

Her mother and grandmother exchanged glances, looking like a couple of conspirators. "Nothing. Just helping you get going."

Her grandmother was studying her as if she hadn't seen her lately. "Don't you think it's time you gave up wearing black? It's over two years now."

Hannah could only stare at her with an open mouth. "What are you…"

"A man who's courting doesn't want to see the woman he cares about looking all washed out," Grossmammi added. "Not that you look washed out, but your green dress makes your eyes look greener."

"She has a nice color in her cheeks anyway," Mammi added.

Hannah opened her mouth and then shut it. It was time she escaped, before they tried to extract any more information than they already seemed to have. She scurried up the stairs, finding herself wondering if that green dress was ready to wear.

For a moment she felt as giddy as a teenager and reminded herself that she was a grown woman with children. That didn't seem to help much, but she went into her bedroom and pulled out the green dress.

Samuel walked to the front windows casually, glancing down the street. No need for Joseph to know he was looking for Hannah's familiar buggy.

"Are Hannah and the boys coming today?" Joseph's voice had a tinge of amusement.

"I'm not sure." He strode back to the machines, wondering why everyone had so much interest in his business. Well, he ought to know by now what it was like living in a small Amish community.

Maybe Hannah was having second thoughts. Maybe she wished she had just said no to him. Maybe...

He'd told himself yesterday that he had to be patient, but his patience seemed to be unraveling. Was this how he'd felt when he'd thought he was in love as a teenager? Oddly enough, he couldn't even recall the girl's face. Despite his conviction that he'd been in love and ready to marry, he had never felt for Ella what he felt now for Hannah. It looked as if Ella had done the right thing in breaking up their relationship. Clearly they hadn't been right for each other.

A clattering at the front door had him swinging back to the front again in time to see the boys rush in at top speed. Will was coming so fast that he barged right into the stack of things Sam had been sorting out for the summer sale days, sending them flying.

"Will." Hannah sounded exasperated. "When are you going to start looking where you're going?"

"Sorry, Mammi. Sorry, Sam. Sam, are you going to put things out for the sidewalk sales? We saw some people putting out tables."

Elijah was already bending to pick up the small leather goods from the floor. Sam turned Will around and pointed. With a grin, Will squatted down and helped his brother. "Are you?" he repeated.

"Will!" Hannah's voice held a warning note, and Sam spoke quickly.

"Yah, we'll put a table out. It's not until Friday, though, so that's time enough to put things out. You can help, okay?"

Hannah smiled, carrying the lunch pails toward the back room. "They were excited about the tables. They may not remember seeing the sidewalk sale before."

As she passed him, Sam couldn't resist clasping her hand just for a moment. He was rewarded when the warm flush touched her cheeks.

No, he hadn't felt like this as a teenager. This was an entirely new and different feeling. Was Hannah thinking the same? Or was she comparing what was between them with her relationship with Jonas? For an instant he actually felt jealous of Jonas, but he chased the idea away. He couldn't let that notion take root or it might spoil everything.

Sam glanced toward the back room, but it probably wasn't a good idea to follow Hannah, much as he would like a few minutes alone with her. He'd said he wouldn't press her for an answer, so he'd best be extra careful.

Hannah came out before he could change his mind again. Starting to say something, he was caught off guard and stood there gaping. Hannah wasn't wearing black today. The deep green of her dress made the blue of her eyes look almost brighter and brought out the color in her cheeks. He'd never seen her look so lovely. The impetuous girl he'd once known had been transformed into a beautiful woman.

She blinked, staring at him, and Sam realized he must look like an idiot, standing there with his mouth open.

"Is something wrong?"

"No...no, of course not." Now he was the one who must be blushing. "I just... I just thought how nice you look today."

Nice, he repeated to himself. Of all the stupid things to say. She didn't look nice, she looked beautiful. What was wrong with him?

Too late. She went on past him to where the boys were checking out the things for the sale table. She bent over them, helping to group the items.

"What else can we do?" As always, Will was eager to rush on to something else.

"If we came early tomorrow morning, we could help set up outside, ain't so?" Elijah looked at Sam as if to draw him back into the conversation.

"Sure, if your mammi says it's all right."

Hannah smiled, nodding. "I guess the boys had better, since they're learning how to be your junior partners."

"And you?" he asked softly, loving the way her eyes laughed at him.

"I guess I could do that."

"Isn't there anything else to get ready now?" Will asked.

He tried to think of something else to provide. He had to admit he'd never been especially eager to participate in the sidewalk sales, but as a merchant, he didn't have much choice.

"There are a couple of boxes up on that top shelf that might have something worth putting out. They hadn't sold, so I packed them away. I'll get them down later."

"If we had a ladder, I could get them," Will said, his head tilted back to eye the boxes. "I could hand them down to Elijah."

Sam instinctively shuddered at the thought of Will up on a ladder.

"No ladders," Hannah said firmly.

"That's right," Sam agreed. "I think Joseph picked up a bag of crullers at the bakery this morning. Go and ask if we can have some for a snack."

The twins darted back toward Joseph, immediately forgetting about ladders, and Hannah laughed. "Good job distracting them. Crullers for the boys is like a handful of oats for the pony—irresistible."

They walked together in the wake of the children. It was a good feeling, being together, working together, guiding the children together. Sam felt his confidence growing. Hannah hadn't said yes, but things were moving that way, weren't they?

Crullers and coffee, with juice for the boys, had everyone relaxing, enjoying each other's company. Like a family, he told himself.

When Hannah stood at the sink, cleaning up, Samuel lingered as the others went back to the shop, thinking of those moments at the sink in the farmhouse kitchen. He let his hand drift over to hers, clasping her wet fingers.

"Have you had a chance to think about us? Are you ready to give me an answer, Hannah?"

She lifted her face, eyes shining, but still a little hesitant. "I think—"

A loud crack from the front of the shop, followed by a shout from Joseph, had him spinning toward the door. He surged into the shop and froze for just an instant. Will clung to the shelf where the boxes were, but the whole shelf unit was shaking, pulling loose from the wall, dislodging the boy. It looked ready to collapse on top of him.

Sam flung himself forward, hurtling over the worktable in his way, his thoughts filled with incoherent prayers.

Hannah was a step or two behind Sam. Her heart pounded furiously at the sight of Will clinging to the top shelf. Elijah scrambled toward his brother, and Sam yelled at him to get back. She was too far away; she'd never reach him in time.

Sam seemed to fly toward him. He jumped, and with one hand he slammed the shelving unit against the wall while the other hand plucked Will from the shelf. Hannah gasped, feeling as if her heart would burst from her chest. Boxes, halters and lead lines fell in a tangle.

Joseph had reached the shelf now, steadying it against the wall. Samuel bent over, feeling Will's arms and legs.

"Do you hurt anywhere?" Sam asked urgently.

Will stifled a sob and shook his head, looking at the chaos around him. "I didn't mean to make a mess. I just wanted to get the box."

"I said I'd get it later, didn't I?" Sam's voice rose. "A mess is right!"

"I'll help—" Will reached toward the mess, but Sam snatched him back.

"Stay away." Sam gave him a swat on the behind. "Go on, get back."

Hannah grabbed her son and pulled him toward her, relief that he was all right mixed with fury at Sam for unleashing his anger on Will.

"That's enough." She held Will close, trying hard to suppress the words that wanted to spill out. She couldn't say what she wanted to right here in the store.

Fortunately, the bell jangled on the door just then, forcing her to swallow her feelings.

It was the Englisch woman who seemed to be a frequent customer. "Looks like an accident," she said, glancing from one to the other of the twins. "I didn't know you had any children, Sam."

"I don't," he snapped, stepping over things to reach her. "What can I do for you?"

That's right, you don't, Hannah thought. *So don't act like you have the right to discipline my children.*

"Go back to the storeroom," she told them quietly. She was about to follow them when Joseph motioned her over to the shelves.

"You want to steady this while I get something to fasten the shelves to the wall? Seems like we should have done it before."

"Yah." She glared toward Samuel, but he was engrossed in his customer. Still, she couldn't refuse to help Joseph. None of it was his fault.

Hannah managed to make her stiff lips smile as she held the shelves in place. She'd do this, and then she'd collect the boys and leave.

"Glad the boy's okay." Joseph interrupted her thoughts. "Boys are like that, yah? Always doing things without thinking of what can go wrong."

"I guess so," she muttered. "My grandfather always says you can't expect to see an old head on young shoulders."

"The bishop should know."

To her relief, Joseph didn't say anything more. He meant to be helpful, but he couldn't. She had to figure this out for herself.

She was grateful to Samuel for his quick action, for sure. He'd saved Will from harm. But he didn't have the right to punish her boys. That was her responsibility.

Maybe it was good that this had happened now. She'd been teetering on the edge of saying yes to him. Did she really want to do that?

She and the twins had a nice, comfortable home with the support of her family. Was she willing to give all that up for the risk of starting a new life with Sam?

"Hannah?"

The sound of Sam's voice startled her. She hadn't realized he was standing so close to her, nor that the Englisch woman had left, and she didn't think she had anything to say to him right now.

She stiffened. "I think we'd better leave now." She turned to go and collect the boys, but he clasped her wrist.

"Not until you tell me what you're thinking."

Hannah stared at him, her anger starting to bubble again. "Let go of me." Her voice was as cold as an icy pond in winter.

He released her, but his face tightened. "That's it? You'll just walk away? Why? Because I was angry with Will for doing something he knew he shouldn't? He came close to hurting himself."

"You yelled at him. You smacked him. You don't have the right to do that. I'm his parent, not you."

His face whitened as if she'd hit him. "If we were to marry, you'd have to let go of that. Will you be able to? Because if not…" He stopped, looking as if he was afraid to go any further.

"I don't know." That was the honest answer. "We'd best leave." She walked away quickly, afraid to say anything else for fear it would be something irrevocable. Sam was right. That was what marriage meant, to share everything, good and bad, as one person. If she wasn't willing to accept that, she couldn't possibly marry him.

Chapter Fifteen

Hannah drove home in silence, afraid of saying anything in front of the twins. Had they heard anything of what she and Sam had said to each other? She didn't think so, but she couldn't be sure.

Probably she should talk to them about it, but the strength had seeped out of her until she could hardly hang onto the reins. She just wanted to get home, get away from everyone and escape into sleep. But she couldn't do that without making everyone fuss over her, wanting to know what was wrong. So she'd just have to keep a good face on. If she could.

"Mammi?" Elijah spoke in a soft voice. "Are you mad at us?"

Hannah pulled herself together. She was letting her feelings for another person affect her relationship with the twins, and that wasn't fair.

"No, Elijah." She swallowed, trying to get the lump out of her throat. "I'm upset with William for doing something so foolish."

Elijah sighed. "You'd better be upset with me, too. I knew he shouldn't, but I didn't tell him to stop."

Will sniffled a little, looking from his brother to her and then studying the floor of the buggy as if he hadn't ever seen it before.

Her instinct told her that something was going on besides what was obvious. "Will? What do you say to that?"

"I shouldn't have climbed on the shelves. I'm sorry."

"Good. You should be." Now that they were talking, Hannah felt not quite so strangled as she had a few minutes ago. "Why did you think that was a good idea?"

The boys looked at each other, and she waited. The pony's hooves echoed hollowly on the road.

"Tell her," Elijah told his brother. "You know. Just tell Mammi."

A glance at Will told her he'd like to do anything else. He swallowed, his throat working. "I didn't mean to make such a mess. Honest, I didn't."

"I know. But I don't know why you did it even so."

It was Elijah who filled in the blanks. "Remember when you told us about how our daadi was climbing and showing off and Sam jumped in and saved him?"

She couldn't say she understood, because she didn't. "What does that have to do with getting out things for tomorrow's sale?"

"Nothing," Will declared, glaring at his brother. "Let me tell it. We thought it would be good to have a daadi again, like the other boys. But it seemed like nothing was happening."

"Will said he'd do like Daadi did in the story," Elijah added.

"And then Sam would save me, and you'd want to marry him, and we'd have Sam for a daadi," Will finished. "But it didn't work." He wiped his face with his fingers, as if to be sure there weren't any tears. "Why didn't it work, Mammi?"

She didn't know. Something grabbed hold of her heart, and she felt panic rip through her.

"I don't know," she managed to say. "But getting married is for two grown-ups to decide. Nobody else. When you get old enough to feel that way, then you get to make that decision. And it's never okay to do something dangerous to make someone do what you want. Understand?"

They both nodded solemnly. Did they really understand? Had she said the right thing? Parenthood seemed stocked with difficult questions. Right or wrong?

She studied their small faces, so alike and yet different. Then Sam's face intruded in her thoughts. Had she been fair to him? She didn't know. It seemed the older she got, the less she knew.

They pulled up at the house, and she prepared herself for all the questions. *Why are you back so soon? Why has Will been crying? What happened?*

Daad came out, and after one look at her, he collected the twins and hustled them off to take care of the pony. She looked after them, but there was no point in interfering. It would all come out anyway. It was impossible to keep secrets in a close family.

Mammi and Grossmammi looked at her, and then her mother poured out a mug of coffee and set it in front of her.

She shook her head. "I just had a coffee." Hadn't she? The morning seemed all jumbled up to her.

"Then I'll take this one." Her grandmother sat down next to her and patted her hand. "What happened? You can tell us."

Her mother nodded, sitting on her other side. "Komm, tell us. Trouble is better shared."

Suddenly she felt surrounded by their love—a good feeling, but somehow almost suffocating right now. She pressed her lips together, trying to resist the temptation to pour it out. She had to say something.

"Nothing... I mean...it wasn't anything." She could feel their gazes on her face, urging her to speak. "The boys got into mischief, and I was upset, and...well, I just decided we would come home."

Hannah stood up, pushing away from the table. "I... I'd better go help the boys." She rushed outside, feeling tears welling that she wasn't going to shed, and walked slowly toward the barn.

The clouds that had been threatening all day grew even darker. They suited her mood. She tried to stoke up her anger—anger seemed better than this heavy sorrow, but she couldn't even do that.

Had she been wrong to react the way she did? Everything she'd said was true. She was responsible for the twins. Everyone in the family helped, but she alone was their mother. How could Sam interfere the way he had? Didn't he realize—

The door from the daadihaus opened, and her grandfather came out. As he walked toward her, he seemed to move more slowly this day. She'd always seen Grossdaadi as an ageless figure, but today he seemed bowed down with responsibility.

He came up to her and took her hand. "Komm, walk with me."

She could walk away from the others, but not

from him. Walking hand in hand, she began to feel like a little girl again, holding onto the bishop, who knew everything and could answer every question. She'd wondered, sometimes, how God spoke to him. In parables, as Jesus did? Or as a voice in the night, like Samuel in the Bible?

They turned down the path that led to the creek, always one of her favorite places, even on a cloudy day like this. They stopped at the flat rock that extended into the creek and looked at the water rippling over the pebbles. The stream was a little lower, as it often was in the summer.

"Something happened with Samuel, yah?"

Her grandfather's question compelled a response, and now she felt as if she wanted to tell him—she wanted to pour it out into his listening ears and listen for his wise answers.

"It was the boys," she started. "Will wanted to help set up for the sale, and instead of waiting for Sam, he started to climb up on the shelves. They shook, pulling away…" Tears spilled over at the image. "I started for him, but Sam got there first. All in a minute he had plucked him down, pushing the shelf back and setting him down."

"He wasn't hurt."

She shook her head. "Sam got to him in time."

"That doesn't sound like anything to make you angry with him," he observed.

"No." She wiped away a tear that had spilled

over. "But then Sam was angry with Will for being so disobedient. He smacked him on the bottom and scolded him." She paused for a moment. "He shouldn't have done that. He's not their father."

"It's what I would have done in his place."

"That's different," she said quickly. "You're his grandfather. You love him."

"Yah. I love him."

Hannah thought he was going to say more, but he didn't. He just left it there, waiting for her to respond.

Instead of whirling out of control, her thoughts had slowed, moving as smoothly as the ripples in the creek. *Love*, he had said. It was love that made the difference.

By the time Hannah had fended off the boys' attempts to go with her, harnessed the pony cart and driven past the porch onto the lane, her mother was on the porch waving at her.

"The rain—" She pointed. "Wait until later."

Hannah shook her head, not stopping. The trees along the lane were already blowing, their leaves turning, announcing the coming rain, and a flicker of lightning gave more evidence. But she couldn't stop, not now that she was sure. She'd walked away from Samuel with bitter words, and goodness knew what he was thinking. The longer this estrangement lasted, the harder it would be to mend, and she wasn't willing to risk that.

A roll of thunder came like a punctuation mark from the other side of the ridge. The mare flung her head up, no doubt smelling the rain in the air and wanting to go back to her comfortable stall.

If she and the mare both got drenched, it didn't matter. She knew what she and the boys needed, and she wouldn't be stopped for anything.

As if she'd challenged the rain, the skies opened. She saw the first drops hitting the ground and then the rain came down in a deluge. Thankful for the shawl she tossed on the seat, Hannah slowed the mare and pulled the thick shawl over her head, kapp and all, as best she could. That would have to do.

She snapped the lines and then pulled up abruptly. A buggy had pulled into the lane from the road...a buggy she recognized. It was Samuel. He drew up and stopped, blocking the road.

He jumped down and ran to her. "What are you doing out in the rain in an open pony cart? You're getting soaked." He held out his hands. "Komm into the buggy. At least you'll be under the roof."

Before she was quite sure what was happening, Samuel had lifted her down and carried her to the buggy, then swung up beside her.

"Where were you going?"

The sharp question didn't bother her in the least, not when she could see the anxiety and caring in his face.

"Where were you?" she countered.

"I thought—" He stopped, pushing a strand of wet hair back from her face. His fingers were warm against her skin. "You're wet and cold," he chided. He picked up the shawl and wrapped it around her shoulders, leaving his arm across her shoulders for a moment before pulling back.

Hannah struggled to put her thoughts in order. She had to tell him what she felt, and how wrong she had been.

"I'm sorry..." she began.

"No, I'm sorry." He touched her lips with his fingers. "I shouldn't have said what I did. Will scared me half to death."

"Me, too. I guess I just had to strike out at someone, but it shouldn't have been you." She tried to read his face. "You said I was impetuous, and that's what I was."

Sam shook his head. "I didn't have the right to—"

"You did," she burst in. "I took me a bit to understand. You had the right, because you love him. Both of them. That's it, isn't it?"

His expression relaxed into a look of such tenderness that her heart turned over. "I love all three of you."

Hannah's heart was so full it seemed about to burst out of her chest. "I was afraid I'd lost you."

"If so…" He shook his head. "I've never been good with people—the girl I was going to marry, Jonas and his father—I kept making the wrong decisions. I couldn't let that happen with you. I'd already hurt you so much."

"Don't think that," she said urgently. "We both made mistakes. We were both afraid of taking the risk. But it's not too late, is it?"

He pressed his cheek against hers. "It can't be. I can't go on without you, Hannah. Marry me. I'll do my best to be the person you and the boys need."

"You already are," she whispered, turning her lips against his.

She drew him closer, feeling his strong arms holding her against him. Love and longing flowed through them. This was right. This was what God had for them all along.

Together, with God's blessings, they would create a new family, not forgetting the past but building on it to enrich the future.

The rain blew in on them, and both horses tossed their heads in disapproval. Samuel chuckled, deep in his chest. "I think they want us to move on. Yah?"

She smiled. "The family will be waiting. We'd best go in before they come after us." She started to slip down to take the reins of the pony cart, but Samuel pulled her back.

"You stay here where you're protected a little." He tucked the shawl more closely around her and hopped down, reaching the pony cart in a few long strides. They headed back to the house and the waiting family, ready to share their happiness with all the people who loved them.

Epilogue

A group of teenagers who'd been chattering outside since the wedding finally came back into the house. For a moment Hannah wondered where they were going to fit, but then she realized it wasn't her responsibility. It was her wedding day, and other people were ready and eager to take over everything that had to be done.

Samuel, reading her thoughts as usual, clasped her hand warmly. "Just relax. It's probably the last time you'll be able to."

She laughed, looking up at her new husband. "I just didn't expect so many people. A second wedding is usually a quiet affair."

"It's the first one for me," he reminded her. "Anyway, besides family and neighbors and friends, every one of the matchmaking group wanted to be here."

She looked around, picking them out in the crowd that milled around the table. Sure enough, they were all there.

"The only match we made was ours," she pointed out.

Even as she spoke, she noticed Katie motioning the group together. Two of the visiting teen boys had come, and she wondered if that was because of Katie. It was impossible to tell just from looking at Dorcas's daughter, who never seemed to be aware of her followers.

Katie tapped on the table, and the busy chatter diminished. "We..." she gestured toward her group "...all wanted to be here to offer our love and best wishes to Hannah and Samuel. We probably gave them a lot of trouble during our events this past summer..." A few teens started to giggle at that. "But despite it all, they never lost patience with us. They are true friends, and we want to thank them."

A round of applause punctuated her words, and Katie's cheeks grew rosy. With a nod to the others, she led a long line of teenagers around the table to shake hands or give hugs and kisses to Hannah and Samuel.

Now it was their turn to be embarrassed. Hannah had to laugh when Katie reached up to kiss Samuel's cheek. He obviously didn't know what to do, and his face grew bright red. Laughing, she clasped his hand.

"We'll be alone sooner or later," she whispered

to him, and he gave her such a loving look that it wrapped her heart in joy.

She'd begun to think they'd actually be able to sit down and have their dessert when Will and Elijah came worming their way though the crowd. Will grabbed Samuel's sleeve and tugged it.

"Grossmammi said that you and Mammi won't be home tonight. Can't we go with you?"

Sam looked at her as if asking her to take that question, and she chuckled again. "You're a daadi now, remember? You get to answer questions like that."

He started to speak, but Elijah got in first, poking his brother. "I told you, silly. They just got married so they want to be by themselves."

Sam stooped to put an arm around each of the boys. "Only for tonight, and then we'll be back, and you'll have us around forever."

Hannah's grandfather came up behind the boys. "That's a gut promise," he said. "I see your grandmother is cutting a chocolate cake. Don't you want some?"

They ran off, and Hannah hugged her grandfather. "We didn't make matches for anyone else, but it certain sure worked for us."

He glanced toward the young ones and smiled. "It's too early to know whether any of them will get together. Time will tell."

"As far as I can tell, it worked out well for the two of us," Samuel said. "Denke. And thank you for your beautiful words at the service."

Hannah nodded, her throat too tight to speak. The bishop usually was part of any wedding in the community, but this one had been special. She'd actually seen his eyes glaze with tears as he said his final words, bringing her to tears.

"We learn a great deal from our first loves," he'd said, putting his hand over their clasped ones. "But it's our last loves that bring us happiness."

* * * * *

Dear Reader,

The book you're reading will probably be the final novel I write. Time marches on, and it becomes more difficult to do all the things I'd like to do. So, thinking this will be the last one (number eighty-eight!), it is especially precious to me.

As this concludes the story arc of the Brides of Lost Creek books, it's appropriate that it's about love…finding love, recognizing love, sharing love. As the Scripture tells us, the greatest of these is love.

I'll be thinking of you, dear friends, as I enter into my retirement.

Blessings,
Marta Perry

We hope you enjoyed
The Amish Matchmakers
by Marta Perry!

Discover all the stories in the heartwarming Brides of Lost Creek miniseries:

Second Chance Amish Bride
The Wedding Quilt Bride
The Promised Amish Bride
The Amish Widow's Heart
A Secret Amish Crush
Nursing Her Amish Neighbor
The Widow's Bachelor Bargain
Match Made at the Amish Inn

Read on for an excerpt from
Match Made at the Amish Inn...

Chapter One

"Molly Esch, if you don't stop fussing over this room for a child you don't even know, I'm going to scream."

Having known Hilda since they were in first grade together at the Amish school, Molly felt sure that Hilda would do no such thing, but now that Hilda was working for her at the Amish Inn, she'd reverted to talking like that sassy six-year-old she'd been. And Hilda wouldn't be content until she had an answer.

"Think of it," Molly said, frowning at the patchwork quilt on the single bed. She'd love to find something more suited to a little girl. "Poor little thing is only eight, and she's lost her mother and she and her daadi are moving to a strange place. I want it to be welcoming for her."

"Ach, I understand that." Hilda's face softened with sympathy. "Poor child," she echoed. "But what about the father? You haven't said a thing about why Leah Fisher wants to bring in this stranger to manage the inn when you've been helping her for over two years and could do it perfectly fine all by yourself. So tell me!"

Hilda's eyes sparkled with curiosity, and her normally sharp voice demanded answers. Everything about Hilda had always been sharp, from her pointed nose to her high voice to her curiosity about anyone and everyone in the community of Lost Creek.

No wonder Hilda wanted to know. Leah Fisher *had* been Molly's friend all her life and her mentor during the two years since Molly's life had crumbled around her. Why had Leah decided to bring in this stranger to take charge of the inn while Leah recovered from her accident?

Leah doesn't trust you to do it. That critical voice in the back of her mind had been unusually active since her intended husband had run off the very night before their wedding.

Leah had been a rock at the time. In the midst of all the gossip and sympathy and wondering, Leah, her mother's dearest friend, had appeared with the most helpful suggestion—that Molly should come and work with her in running the Amish Inn.

Molly had to smile at Leah's idea of a cure for a broken heart—work, challenge and more work. But it had turned out just as her mother and Leah had expected. Learning all the ins and outs of running the busy inn and catering to the mostly Englisch visitors had given her a new interest in life. Gradually Leah had put more and more of the actual management into Molly's hands, challenging her, and Molly had been so occupied that she hadn't had time to mourn over William's defection to the outside world.

Molly had thought Leah had confidence in her, and her own self-confidence, battered as it had been, had begun to come back. But now, when Leah had to turn the management over to someone else while her badly broken legs healed, she'd brought in her husband's nephew to do it instead of relying on Molly.

She doesn't trust you. Molly wondered if hitting her head against the stairwell wall would quiet that voice in her mind. Dismissing the impulse, she and Hilda went down the back stairway of the inn's annex, where the owner lived. Maybe Hilda had given up on her questioning, but she doubted it.

"Well?" Hilda demanded as they emerged into the kitchen from the narrow stairway. "Why is she bringing in this Aaron Fisher?"

Molly shrugged, knowing she had to say something or Hilda never would go home. Aaron Fisher and his little daughter would be here before long, and she needed a few minutes to tidy herself.

But it looked as if she wasn't going to get them. The front doorbell rang, and then Leah called out to her.

"Molly, they're here!" Leah sounded so excited that Molly knew she had to move fast before Leah was trying to get out of bed.

"I'll be right there," Molly called. She shoved Hilda out the back door with questions still on her lips. "I'll tell you when I figure it out," she said. "See you tomorrow."

She closed the door on Hilda's protests, dusted off her apron and tidied her hair as best she could. Then she hurried toward the front door, where the bell was ringing again.

She risked a glance out the front window to see an Englisch driver unloading suitcases and bags from a station wagon, while an Amish man and child stood on the porch. Yah, that would be Aaron Fisher. Now she had to wilkom him and act as if nothing at all was wrong. Taking a deep breath, she arranged a smile on her face and opened the door.

Molly decided she might as well not have bothered about the smile, since the man who must be Aaron Fisher clearly didn't. In fact, his face wore no expression at all. If he was glad to be here, it didn't show.

Still, she recognized him. She'd seen him long ago, when Aaron had visited his aunt and uncle as a teenager, and she'd been a little girl tagging along with her mother. Then he'd looked…superior, she decided. At that point, she hadn't dared to talk to him.

But times had changed. She slid a strand of bronze hair back under her kapp. One thing about having red hair—folks usually remembered you. But it seemed that Aaron didn't.

"Wilkom, Aaron." She infused a little extra pleasure into her voice to make up for the fact that she didn't feel it. He was looking back toward the driver and the luggage and didn't immediately respond. In fact, he almost seemed to look past the driver, toward the place he'd left. She felt a surge of sympathy that surprised her.

"Please, come in," she said, gesturing to the hallway of the annex. "And this must be Rebecca." She bent to bring her face on the level of the eight-year-old, who edged behind her father, holding onto his black coat. "Do you like to be called Becky?"

She didn't get a smile. The child's bright blue eyes just stared at her warily. The freckled little face seemed made for laughter, not for the solemn expression it wore now.

Still, she guessed there was no reason why a motherless eight-year-old should be happy about yet another change in her short life. After a moment, the little girl gave the slightest nod.

Relieved, Molly smiled again as she straightened, but Aaron's expression, or lack of it, hadn't changed. "Is that my aunt?" he asked abruptly.

Yanked back to the here and now, Molly realized she was hearing the tinkling sound of the small bell Leah used to let her know she wanted something.

"Yah, they're here," she called out. "Do you want them to come to you first, before dealing with the luggage?"

Leah's cheerful laugh sounded. "For sure. I need a hug from my kinfolk."

"Right away, then." She pointed to the open door that led to the former dining room, now converted into a room for a recuperating patient.

"Your aunt is just in there. Do you want—"

He didn't let her finish. Holding his child's hand, he took a long step toward the door. "Tell the driver to put things on the porch. I'll be there to help him in a moment."

Not even a *please*. Somehow, she didn't think Aaron had changed much from that superior teenager who hadn't seemed to see anything he liked in Lost Creek.

She watched as the tall, broad-shouldered man and the tiny child walked away from her. At the last second before entering the other room, Becky turned her head and gave Molly a shy, sweet smile.

She was such a pushover for a child, Molly told herself. Not the father—she could do without him. But she promptly lost her heart to the lonely little girl.

***

Aaron followed his daughter's gaze for a moment, noticing her slight smile. If Becky warmed up to Aunt Leah's helper, that would be more than he'd hoped for. But he didn't have time to think about it now. The woman vanished on her errand, and Aaron turned to find Aunt Leah holding out her arms to him.

He hurried to hug her, but he was shocked. He'd always seen Aunt Leah as an energetic, positive woman, busy every minute of the day. To find her leaning back on her pillows, looking helpless, struck him in the heart. He managed to smile as he pulled away, and she clung to him as if she didn't want to let go. Then her hands slipped away, and he patted her cheek.

"Ach, it's been too long. I've missed you so very much."

"Me, too," he murmured, thinking about the clash between his father and Aunt Leah's husband. How any two brothers could have been so different, he didn't know, but it had created a chasm between the two families. Maybe now that breach could be healed.

"I know." Aunt Leah seemed to understand exactly what he thought. "They were too different in so many ways, but they were certain sure alike in their stubborn insistence that they were right."

"They were, always." He looked back with sorrow at the split between the families. Everyone had been hurt by it, but his daad and his onkel never seemed to see it.

"Well, they're both gone now," Aunt Leah said with some of her usual spirit. "Their quarrel died with them, and they're at peace. It's time to move on."

"You're right," he said firmly. He wouldn't hold on to a grudge he'd never understood.

"I wanted to find a way to get you here, but I didn't count on this." She gestured to the bulky casts on both her legs.

"No, that's certain sure." He sat back in the chair by the bed, holding Becky in the curve of his arm. "How did it happen?"

"Ach, I was foolish, that's certain sure. Molly told me not to venture down the cellar steps, but I didn't listen to her." She made a face. "It was a long way to that cement floor. If Molly had already left, I'd have been down there all night."

"It sounds as if you should have listened to her advice." Surely that woman could have prevented Leah's foolishness if she'd tried.

"I was never very good at heeding advice," she said, her soft cheeks crinkling in a smile. "Anyway, I'm wonderful glad you were able to come. I was so afraid you wouldn't be able to."

Her letter had actually been a gift from the Lord to Aaron, though she couldn't know it. It had given him a reason to leave behind the place where his wife had died, the place that reminded him of his loss every second of every day.

"It was the best thing that could have happened for us." He gave Becky a little hug. "We were ready to be somewhere for a fresh start. Right, Becky?"

He looked at her sweet face. It used to be so lively and energetic, filled with happiness and curiosity. Now it seemed he couldn't find the child she'd been. She'd pulled back into a shell, and he hadn't been able to reach her. Maybe now it would be different.

Maybe. Right now it didn't seem likely, but there was time—time to get used to a new place, new people, relatives who would love her.

Aunt Leah gave an understanding smile, as if she understood everything he didn't say.

At that moment, there was a light tap on the door, which stood open. The woman his aunt had called Molly hesitated there, as if wondering if she were welcome.

"I'm sure you have lots to catch up on, but I wondered if Becky would like to see her new bedroom and put some of her things away." Her smile was for Becky.

"I don't think..." he began, sure that Becky wouldn't go anywhere without him. To his astonishment, she pulled away from the circle of his arm, nodding. He touched her shoulder. "Are you sure?"

Becky nodded vigorously.

"Yah, all right, then. You mind what Molly says now."

She nodded and went carefully around the bed to take the hand Molly held out to her. With a quick glance backward, she hurried out of the room. He could hear their steps on the stairs and the light sounds of their voices. He pictured them talking to each other, Molly's green eyes sparkling. That dark red hair like the center of a flame… Where had he seen it before?

Aunt Leah laughed a little. "You're surprised, ain't so?"

"I am surprised," he responded. "Becky never warms up to new people that fast. At least not since her mammi passed."

"Ach, it's a hard thing for a child her age. But you'll see. Molly is good with people, especially kinder. And she knows everything about the inn. Anything you want to know, Molly can tell you." She leaned back on the pillows as if fatigue had swept over her.

"This has been too much for you," he said, clamping down his irritation toward Molly, who knew everything. "Why don't you rest?"

"No, no," Aunt Leah said, though she did look tired. "There's something else I must tell you."

"Maybe later, when you're rested," he suggested.

"No, now." She gripped his hand. "There's something I must say so you'll understand why I wanted you to come now."

He patted her hand. "It's all right. I understand. You wanted some family here to help."

She smiled, her head moving restlessly against the pillow. "Not just that. You have to understand what we planned."

"We?"

"Your Onkel Isaiah," she said firmly. "We talked it over long ago, when we knew we weren't going to have any kinder of our own." Her face seemed drawn for a moment. "It was a grief to us, but there was you. Isaiah's own nephew, and such a fine, loving boy. We decided then that when we were gone, the Amish Inn would belong to you."

It took a few moments for the words to sink in. He'd accepted that she'd needed him during this emergency, but he'd never expected anything like this, especially after the brothers' quarrel.

"You don't mean it," he said. Wondering what exactly he felt about it. If his dear Rachel were still alive…

"Ach, I know exactly what I mean." Her voice was strong. "It was my wish as well as Isaiah's. I just never thought the time would come so soon."

"But you'll get well," he said quickly. "You'll be fine, and you can take charge again. I'll stay as long as you need me, but you can't just give it up. I know how much the inn means to you."

"Yah, it does, but I'm getting tired. I think it's time to ease off a bit. Even if I get back to how I was before the accident, I'd want that. Maybe we'll do it together for a few years. But I'll step back and let you take over."

Aaron still couldn't find the right words. Now that he began to get used to the idea, he found it was increasingly appealing. A thriving business was nothing to turn down. It would be a challenge, but he could feel himself rising to meet it.

"But what about Molly?" he said suddenly. "Wouldn't she be expecting something after working with you?"

"There will be something for Molly, if everything works out." Aunt Leah's lips quirked in a smile, and she seemed to be looking into the future. "I know it. And what do you say?"

Aaron held his breath for a moment, feeling his head spin. If this was what his aunt wanted, how could he turn away from a secure future for his daughter? He let out a long breath. "Yah, all right. If it's what you really want."

Becky held on to Molly's hand on the way up the stairs to the second floor, and the closer they got to the top, the tighter her grip became. Molly looked down at the top of the child's head, seeing the silky hair parted in the middle and drawn back under a snowy kapp. Even the top of her head seemed to announce her tension.

Deciding she'd better break the silence, Molly gestured toward the space around them, where they could glance down at the hall. "This part of the house is called the annex. It's where your Aunt Leah lives. And you, too, now that you're here. The big part in front is where the visitors stay."

Did the child understand? Most eight-year-olds here in Lost Creek would know what she meant, but it was all strange to Becky.

"A lot of strangers?" she asked, looking up at her, and her eyes were wide. A little afraid, Molly thought, of all those Englischers she was imagining.

She paused, turning to smile down at the child. "You know what your Aunt Leah always says? She says strangers are just friends you haven't met yet. All our visitors turn out to be friends."

Becky seemed to puzzle that over in her mind. "Why do they?"

"Mostly because they like it here. And also because your Aunt Leah is so friendly. When she smiles, no one can help but smile back." It occurred to Molly that Becky had only seen her elderly aunt lying in a bed with lines of strain on her face. That hadn't been a good example, she guessed. She tried to think of something else the child might respond to.

"This is the second floor, where the bedrooms are." Molly couldn't help herself... She was eager to see how Becky reacted to her new bedroom. She and Hilda had done their best to make it welcoming to a child.

"See, this first room is usually Aunt Leah's, but she had to move downstairs when she hurt her legs. The next one is for your daadi." She pushed the door farther open and gestured toward the double bed with the patchwork quilt.

Turning, she led Molly across the hall. "And right across from Daadi's room is a bedroom just for you." She flung open the door, hoping the room was as appealing to the child as she'd tried to make it.

But Becky wasn't looking inside. Instead, she gazed at Molly...looking a little lonely, it seemed to her. "But where do you sleep?"

Molly took her hand again, touched by this sign of friendship. "I usually sleep at home, where my mammi and daadi and the rest of the family live. But sometimes I stay here, in case your Aunt Leah needs something in the night."

"Oh." Still a bit of disappointment in her face, and Molly wondered again what was going on in Becky's mind.

Molly led her into the bedroom. "When I was a little girl, I sometimes would sleep here, in the bed you have. My mammi worked at the inn, and she'd bring me with her. So if it was late, she'd tuck me up in this comfy bed." She pressed down on the mattress, and a moment later Becky did the same, seeming to assess its softness.

"You know the story about the three bears?"

Becky nodded, leaning against the end of the bed. "Mammi used to tell me that story." Her lower lip quivered, but then she firmed it, and Molly pretended not to notice.

"I always thought this bed was like the one belonging to Baby Bear. Just right. Maybe it'll be just right for you."

Becky's lips twitched, and then it happened— she smiled. The smile lit her small face with life and enjoyment, and it warmed Molly's heart. That was exactly what she'd hoped for. She could only pray that nothing would happen to disturb the fragile friendship that had sprung up between them.

Becky patted the bed again, and then looked around. "Where do my dresses go?"

"We should have some hooks up for clothes, ain't so? But we have something else here." She ran her fingers down the chair rail molding on the wall and then put Becky's hand on the latch that was almost invisible against the wood. "Just push down on that and see what you find."

For an instant the child looked wary, as if fearing an unpleasant surprise, but then she seemed to gain encouragement from Molly's smile. She pressed, and the door swung open, showing the closet with hooks for clothing. The side wall was lined with shelves, and on them were a few books and toys that Molly had brought from home.

Becky's lips formed a silent O as she looked at the faceless Amish doll who wore a neat kapp that matched her own and a green dress with a white apron. She looked at Molly with a wordless question, and Molly nodded.

"She's for you." Molly lifted her down. "I always thought some little girl who needed a friend might stay here. So that's why she's for you." She smiled, first at the doll and then at Becky, who giggled. Her arms closed around the doll, and then she hesitated.

"For sure?" she asked.

Molly laughed. "For sure. I always called her Maggie, but you can give her another name if you want."

"Maggie," Becky said softly, and hugged the doll close to her heart.

It was a perfect moment, Molly thought. Becky felt welcomed, just as she'd hoped. As for Aaron and the inn—

A deep voice spoke from the doorway. "I thought you were up here unpacking."

Molly tried to hang on to her moment of pleasure, but it slipped away in the withering effect of Aaron's frown. She pinned a smile to her face.

"We're in no hurry. I want to show Becky all the special things about this room that I found when I was her age."

Meanwhile, Becky was tugging at her father's coat. "That's my bed. Molly used to sleep in it sometimes, and she said it was like Baby Bear's bed—just right."

Aaron bent over his daughter, and for a moment Molly couldn't guess what he was thinking. But then he straightened, holding her in his arms, and they smiled at each other, bringing to life a surprising likeness that she hadn't seen before. Her heart seemed to swell in her chest, and for an instant she couldn't breathe.

Then Aaron turned to her, his frown returning. "I'm sure you have other work to do."

They stood there staring at each other. Did he realize how rude that sounded? She couldn't tell. His expression didn't give away his feelings, assuming he had any.

She would do what Leah had asked her to do. But she really couldn't believe that this situation was going to turn out well for her, not when she had to work with...no, work for...a man like this.

Chapter Two

Why did Leah bring in Aaron Fisher? Molly found that Hilda's question kept repeating in her thoughts as she went back downstairs and through the hallway to the inn. She had several guest rooms to freshen up in preparation for visitors in a couple of days. That should give her a little thinking time. Once the tourists started coming for the autumn color, there'd be no time for anything but to keep up.

Hardly noticing what she was doing, she went up the gracious staircase that served the inn itself, running her hand along the highly polished railing. The afternoon sun sent colors through the stained-glass window at the top, and she lingered to admire them. And then she found that her mind had tumbled back to the same place. Aaron was Leah's late husband's kin. Despite the fact that Leah hadn't seen him for years, she'd sent for him to take over management of the inn instead of trusting Molly. No matter how she added it up, Molly still came up with the same answer. Leah didn't trust her to handle it.

Molly realized she'd been standing in the same spot, staring at colors reflecting on the carpet as if she wanted to change the pattern, for at least ten minutes. *Not helping*, she scolded herself. She ought to tackle the problem logically. What did she actually know about Aaron Fisher?

Not much. Leah had been secretive about her thoughts and plans since the accident. Molly's mother might know more—she and Leah had always been close—but if so, she hadn't shared with Molly.

Molly had that vague memory of a superior-looking teenager, coupled with the fact that he was now a widower with a small child. Before she could figure out how to work with him, she'd have to know more. Otherwise, she risked stepping into one pothole after another, saying all the wrong things. Leah would have to talk.

Another fifteen minutes and she was ready to go with the rooms clean and ready except for tomorrow's flowers. She'd best check in on Leah. Molly stiffened her backbone, but her determination turned out not to be needed. As soon as she entered Leah's room, Leah reached out a hand to her.

"Ach, Molly, just the person I wanted to see. We need to talk." Propped up against her stacked pillows, her gray hair still neatly tucked under her kapp the way Molly had fixed it this morning, Leah seemed to have regained a little of her normal color. Perhaps she had taken a short nap after talking with her nephew. She seemed to need more catnaps these days.

"Just what I was thinking." Molly scooted a chair closer to the bed. "I need to know a little more about—"

"About Aaron," Leah finished for her. "Yah, for sure you do. And I need to tell you." She paused, as if thinking her way back through the years, choosing what to share. "First off, Aaron's father was my Isaiah's younger brother. You maybe knew that, but you probably didn't know that the two brothers always seemed to be at odds." She shrugged. "Maybe they were just too much alike—both as stubborn as the day is long."

Molly nodded to show she understood, but she was wondering what this ancient history had to do with today's problems.

"Aaron was the first of his generation in the family, and, as it turned out, the only one." Sorrow creased her face for a moment, and Molly knew why. The grief of Leah's life had been the fact that she had no child of her own.

Leah shook her head, as if shaking off those painful memories. "So Isaiah always said that if the inn was a success, we would leave it to

Aaron." She hesitated, and then went on, studying Molly's face. "I'm bound by that promise, and it's always been my wish, as well, for the inn to stay in the family. But I'll need your help to make it happen."

"For sure," Molly said quickly. "I understand. And I'll help all I can. I promise." At least it wasn't a question of her competence or of Leah's trust in her. Leah was counting on her to prepare Aaron for his inheritance.

Relief swept through her, but it was tinged with a fear of inadequacy. It wasn't that she doubted her knowledge where running the inn was concerned. But how could she help Aaron if he didn't listen to a word she said?

Leah was already sweeping on. "Isaiah and I thought that as Aaron grew, we'd gradually teach him how to run things, but we didn't count on Isaiah's quarrel with his brother taking off the way it did." She shook her head gravely. "Mind, it was Isaiah's fault, too, but neither of them would give an inch. If only..."

She let that trail off, seeming to drift into thoughts of the past. At last, she sucked in a deep breath and gave Molly a determined look. "Ach, it's no use dwelling on what we ought to have done. We must just pick up and move on. That's what I must do, with your help, ain't so?"

"I'll do my best." She'd best air her concerns

now. "You'll have to help me, because I don't know Aaron very well. He probably doesn't see any good reason why he should listen to me."

Leah nodded. "Poor boy," she murmured. "Ach, I wish I'd seen him more often. He's changed so much since his wife died, and I've missed it all."

"It's been what? A year or two?" Molly remembered hearing Leah talk about it, but since she hadn't known them, it hadn't made much impression on her.

"Just about a year and a half, I think." Leah's forehead wrinkled in an effort to clear her thoughts, something that seemed more difficult since her accident. "Yah, it was in the early spring last year. It's hard, not having more family. His father had passed, and his mother moved to Ohio to live with her sister."

"That's unusual...for an Amish person not to have family around to help them, I mean," Molly said. "Especially hard for a father left alone with a child." She found herself picturing Becky's sad little face and how it lit up at the sight of her daadi.

They must have a good relationship together, didn't they? Perhaps Aaron just didn't know how to help Becky with her grief. That happened, sometimes.

"I blame myself," Leah said. "I should have invited them to come here right after it happened. I could have helped. Even if Aaron held on to his father's grudge against us, I should…"

"Aren't you the person who just told me not to look at the past?" Molly patted her hand. "Just pick up the day's burden and move ahead, yah?"

For a moment, Molly feared she'd offended her, but then Leah chuckled softly. "That's right, Molly. You just quote my own words back to me whenever I need to hear them." She squeezed Molly's hand. "You're just like your mammi, with a heart full of love."

A heart full of love that Will hadn't wanted, Molly found herself thinking. She wasn't a good person to help someone else grieving a lost love, but she seemed to be the only one handy. It was certain sure Leah thought she could do it.

Her thoughts slid off in another direction. "After a year and a half, well… I'd think there might be someone else in Aaron's community looking to step into his wife's place."

"For sure, there must be," Leah said. "But Aaron seems to have closed himself off from anyone who might care for him and Becky." She shook her head, staring absently at their linked hands. "Just remember that I'm relying on you."

A sound from behind her made Molly take a glance in that direction. Aaron stood in the doorway. He stared at her with a look as cold as an icicle.

* * *

Aaron froze where he stood. How could he freeze, when inside a fire was raging? They'd been talking about him, that was obvious. About his Rachel. He wouldn't have believed it of Aunt Leah. As for Molly, he didn't know enough to say, but not his aunt.

"Komm." Aunt Leah gestured to him, urging him inside. "We were just talking about how we can make Becky feel at home. Molly knows more about eight-year-olds than I do, so she'll be a big help."

He stepped forward, but it wasn't so easy to thaw. "I'm not looking for help." He cut off the words, hoping his tone would discourage both of them from meddling.

"Ach, Aaron, you never know what you might come to need." Aunt Leah seemed unembarrassed at being caught talking about him, and he suspected she wouldn't be easy to discourage.

She was his kin. Did he really want to discourage her? The answer was obviously no. He'd longed to have family around since Rachel died. Well, now he did, and he was reminded that it had its drawbacks.

He forced himself to smile and steered the talk firmly in a different direction. "I came in to talk to my aunt about school for my daughter," he said. "If you'll excuse us…"

Maybe Aunt Leah wasn't embarrassed, but Molly's cheeks were flushed. "Yah, I have things to do."

She looked glad to escape, but his aunt's voice stopped her.

"No, stay here, Molly."

Molly sent him an apologetic look and came back.

"As I said, Molly knows what's what where eight-year-olds are concerned. And she certain sure knows more about the Amish school. Don't you, Molly?"

"I don't know about that, but I do have four younger brothers and sisters, including eight-year-old twins. I guess I can answer any questions you have. With all the talking our Dorie does, I should know a lot."

"Dorie is the girl twin," Aunt Leah explained, her lips twitching. "She's a real chatterbox."

His face twisted as he tried to smile. Becky had been a chatterbox, too, but not now. Not since she lost her mammi.

Aaron realized suddenly that Molly's eyes were focused on his face, and they were filled with understanding and caring. For a moment, he was disoriented. She couldn't know what he was thinking, could she?

"I'm sure Dorie would like to be Becky's friend and show her the school," Molly said.

"Maybe we could get them together over the weekend."

"Maybe," he said slowly, reluctant to commit himself. "But first I want to visit the school and talk to the teacher about my daughter." He didn't mean to sound ungrateful, did he? It seemed to come out that way.

Once again, his aunt rushed in with the answers. He didn't remember her being quite so bossy when Onkel Isaiah was alive.

"That will work out fine," she said. "Tomorrow morning, Hilda will be here helping, so Molly can show you the way to school and introduce you to the teacher." She grimaced. "No one will let me be alone anymore. Makes me feel like a baby."

He was about to say something sympathetic, but Molly just smiled. "If you insist on trying to go down the cellar steps—"

"Ach, I know, I know." Aunt Leah chuckled. "Molly won't let me feel sorry for myself, either."

"Doctor's orders," Molly said brightly. "No moping allowed, according to Dr. Wainwright."

"He sounds like he understands my aunt." Aaron tried to share their gentle teasing, and it wiped out some of the discomfort that had been in the air. "If Molly says it's okay with her, then we'll go chat with the teacher tomorrow."

He certain sure didn't need Molly's help to talk

to the Amish schoolteacher, but it was simpler to agree than to dispute it. Aunt Leah was probably fretting about all the things she couldn't do, like going to the schoolhouse with him tomorrow.

He hesitated, but there was something else on his mind that he ought to work on. "Now that we have that settled, how about letting me pitch in with what needs to be done here? That's why I came, ain't so?"

"We don't have any visitors coming until Saturday." Aunt Leah looked perplexed. "What else would you do?"

"Anything." He waved his hand. "I've learned how to cook a little, and I can clean." He picked up the calendar that was propped on the bedside table. "I see Molly is written in for tonight, but there's no need for her to stay. I'll do whatever needs doing."

He wasn't sure what he'd said, but his aunt and Molly both stared at him for a moment. Then Aunt Leah's lips twitched. "Molly, take him away and explain. I'm ready to have a little nap."

He opened his mouth to argue, but Molly took his arm firmly and led him out of the room, saying, "Have a good rest."

Just before the door closed completely, he distinctly heard a giggle from the direction of the bed. He swung toward Molly to find her laughing, too.

"What is so funny?" He was on the edge of being offended. They were laughing at him, ain't so?

"Ach, Aaron, don't look so solemn." Molly managed to control her laughter, but her eyes still twinkled. "It's just that the person who stays for the night has to help Leah bathe and get ready for bed and so on. It doesn't matter how much she loves you, but she doesn't want you doing that."

"Oh, right." A flow of red washed up to her cheeks, and suddenly he was smiling, too. They stood there for a moment, laughing together, and he felt the barrier between them had crumbled to dust.

The next morning, Aaron seemed filled with energy and eager to get off to the schoolhouse. Molly tried to look equally enthusiastic, but she suspected her tiredness showed through. She'd slept on the camp bed set up in the corner of Leah's room, but *slept* hadn't exactly been the right word for it. What with listening for Leah, ready to jump up at her call and thinking about how she would deal with Aaron over the coming weeks, she hadn't actually spent much of the night sleeping.

She finished washing the breakfast dishes and hung the damp towel over the rack. The inn would go to Aaron when Leah was ready to let it go—that was plain. Well, that was what anyone would expect. He was her husband's only relative.

That was as it should be. The little Leah had told her about Aaron's marriage had increased her sympathy for both Aaron and his daughter. Theirs had been a true love match—what she had thought she had with William. It hurt her heart just to think about Aaron's loss, but it was pointless to say that she knew how he felt. She didn't, and if Leah thought Molly knew what to say in comfort, she was on the wrong track. Leah herself would be far better at that.

Molly leaned against the windowsill and spotted Aaron coming from the barn to the house. She realized, watching him from a distance, that he was huskier than either her closest brother or her daad. A bit taller, too, she'd guess, with a sturdy frame that looked strong enough for anything. She remembered hearing Leah say that he'd worked construction before his wife died. He looked more suited to that than to managing the inn.

He'd obviously finished the chores, and he'd be eager to get off to the school. But not until Hilda arrived, she reminded herself. They couldn't go off and leave Becky alone with Leah.

Her thoughts were interrupted by Becky coming in from her great-aunt's room. She was carrying a child's teapot, and she held it up to Molly.

"Aunt Leah says can you put some tea in my teapot?" Becky asked. "We're going to have a tea party when you and Daadi go to school."

She looked a little doubtful about the whole thing, making Molly wonder if they were in for tears when Daadi tried to leave without her.

"Yah, of course. I'll fix it for you." This was probably Leah's idea of distracting the child, and she smiled down at the little girl. "Would you like to have some snickerdoodles, too?"

Becky's eyes lit up. "If that's okay. Do you think Aunt Leah would like them?"

"I'll tell you a secret," she said, taking the lid off the cookie jar. "Snickerdoodles are your Aunt Leah's favorite cookies. My mamm made these for her."

"They're my favorite, too," Becky whispered. "I'm good at keeping secrets."

Denke, Lord, Molly murmured in her heart, glad that even something as simple as a favorite cookie brought a smile to that solemn little face.

Aaron came in just then, holding the door for Hilda, who was chattering away a mile a minute. For an instant, Molly regretted not having Hilda's gift of gab, but seeing the slightly dazed expression on Aaron's face, she thought the better of it. She'd rather be herself, she decided.

Hilda jumped right into the tea-party plan. She enlisted Aaron's help to move a small table next to Leah's bed, and she and Becky drew up the chairs. Molly brought the teapot and plate of cookies, eyeing Becky to be sure she wasn't getting upset, but she seemed completely engrossed in the tea party. Such a good idea of Leah's, as if she knew instinctively that this was the right thing to do. Perhaps it had been something Becky's mother did with her.

But Leah had always been like that, seeming to know what a child needed. It was so sad that God had not blessed her with a houseful of her own.

She lingered, but Aaron gestured to her impatiently. As soon as they were out of the room, he grasped her arm and hustled her out the back door. His long strides ate up the ground, and Molly had to hurry to keep up with him. Finally, she just stopped. He turned to look at her in annoyance, but then his expression faded into a smile.

"Was I rushing you?" he asked, not looking in the least sorry.

"Just a bit," she said, setting a more moderate pace. "Besides, you were about to go the wrong way."

Aaron flushed a bit, looking annoyed again. He didn't like to be caught in a mistake, she guessed.

Ignoring it, she pointed to the path beyond the

barn that led down to a farm lane. "The children aren't allowed to go along the road. This path leads into the lane. It winds along parallel to the road and ends up at the school."

"Without crossing the road?" He gave a short nod. "Good idea." After a few minutes of walking, he spoke again, sounding more normal now. "Tell me about the school. And the teacher. You went there, ain't so?"

"Well, I went there, so I think it's great, of course. But I would, wouldn't I?" She smiled, inviting him with a look to respond with something about his own school, but he didn't respond, so she went on.

Matching her steps to his, Molly told him about the schoolhouse. She knew it so well after her years there, but it was surprisingly hard to describe it to someone else. Maybe she still saw it with a child's eyes.

"The teacher has changed now, of course. It's Teacher Grace, one of the Miller family. She finished school just a year before I did, and she's been teaching for several years." Molly hesitated. "She's good, you know. Kind and gentle in spirit, but able to control the most obstreperous boys with a look and a word."

"Even all the redheaded Esch children?" he asked, teasing a little and making her lips quirk.

"Yah, even them. Matthew, he's the next

brother after me—he could usually talk his way out of anything, but not with Teacher Grace. She saw right through him." She chuckled. "We enjoyed that."

It wasn't a long walk to the schoolhouse, but it was a pleasant one with willow trees and river birch shading the path. On a warm day like this one, with Aaron trying to be nice, Molly actually enjoyed it despite her initial reluctance.

Just now he was looking between the trees to the right, where a few scattered houses gave way to pastureland. A few placid-looking Herefords raised their heads to look at them before going back to munching.

Molly pointed. "Our farm is the next place off to the left."

He didn't seem interested, so she went on. "There's the school, on the right." Molly turned onto the well-worn path, very conscious of Aaron right behind her. "Teacher Grace will be delighted to have a new scholar, especially one starting so early in the school year."

"I'm more worried about how Becky will take it. She's always liked school, but going to a new place might be different." His voice seemed lower, and she glanced back at him as the path came out on the lawn around the schoolhouse. She saw worry tightening the lines around his eyes and tried to sound optimistic.

"Don't borrow trouble. My daad always says that when my mamm gets het up about something. I didn't understand when I was younger, but I grew to think it's good advice."

His face was still set. "Yah, but it's easier said than done."

"I know," Molly said gently, wishing she saw some softening in his expression. "But if she liked school before, surely she will still like it now. And my little sister Dorie is determined to be her very best friend."

Aaron managed a smile. "Denke, Molly."

Maybe she should warn him about Dorie, who talked even faster than Hilda, if that was possible. But he'd soon see. They reached the steps to the white frame schoolhouse, and Molly paused and turned to him. "They'll be having morning recess in a few minutes, so that will be a good time to talk to Teacher Grace. We'll just wait in the back until then." Since he seemed to accept that, she opened the door and they slipped inside.

Teacher Grace glanced up with a quick smile and continued pointing out something on a map to the older scholars while the younger ones practiced printing their letters. A wave of remembering swept over Molly as they stood waiting at the back. Nothing much had changed over the years, with the same maps pinned up on the board, the same rows of wooden desks and even what looked like the same yellow-and-orange paper leaves pinned around the calendar on the bulletin board.

Molly glanced at Aaron and saw him picking out the three redheads in the classroom—Dorie and David, the eight-year-old twins, and Lida, the eleven-year-old. Lida kept her eyes on the teacher, but Dorie and David stole a quick glance at Molly and Dorie wiggled, as if finding it hard to sit still. Molly gave a tiny shake of the head to her little sister, not wanting to be embarrassed.

Fortunately, the lesson soon came to an end. Teacher Grace put her pointer down unhurriedly, smiling at her pupils. "I'm going to dismiss you for recess in just a moment, but first I want to remind you to be on your best behavior. We have guests today. No, don't stare at them," she ordered as heads swiveled. "Just put your things away and then file out, youngest grades first."

A soft buzz of conversation rose, and Aaron stepped back as the first and second graders came down the center aisle, the boys jostling each other and the girls chattering. Molly moved to the side, hoping Aaron wouldn't get trampled.

Dorie burst out of the crowd, headed for her, stepping on other scholars' feet as she came. As soon as she was close enough, she grabbed Molly's hand and clung tight. Words burst out of her.

"Molly, do you know what Sally Byler said?

She said that her brother William was coming back! I told her he couldn't. How could he come back after running away the night before your wedding? He couldn't, could he?"

Molly froze, feeling Dorie's hand clutching hers and seeing the indignation in her eyes. That was probably what she should feel, too, but instead it was like the time she'd fallen from the apple tree and landed flat on her stomach—the breath knocked out of her so hard that she couldn't even gasp.

Match Made at the Amish Inn
and more titles by Marta Perry
are available now from Love Inspired!

www.LoveInspired.com

Copyright © 2025 by Martha P. Johnson

Get up to 4 Free Books!

We'll send you 2 free books from each series you try PLUS a free Mystery Gift.

FREE Value Over $25

Both the **Love Inspired®** and **Love Inspired® Suspense** series feature compelling novels filled with inspirational romance, faith, forgiveness and hope.

YES! Please send me 2 FREE novels from the Love Inspired or Love Inspired Suspense series and my FREE gift (gift is worth about $10 retail). After receiving them, if I don't wish to receive any more books, I can return the shipping statement marked "cancel." If I don't cancel, I will receive 6 brand-new Love Inspired Larger-Print books or Love Inspired Suspense Larger-Print books every month and be billed just $7.19 each in the U.S. or $7.99 each in Canada. That is a savings of 20% off the cover price. It's quite a bargain! Shipping and handling is just 50¢ per book in the U.S. and $1.25 per book in Canada.* I understand that accepting the 2 free books and gift places me under no obligation to buy anything. I can always return a shipment and cancel at any time by calling the number below. The free books and gift are mine to keep no matter what I decide.

Choose one: ☐ **Love Inspired Larger-Print** (122/322 BPA G36Y)   ☐ **Love Inspired Suspense Larger-Print** (107/307 BPA G36Y)   ☐ **Or Try Both!** (122/322 & 107/307 BPA G36Z)

Name (please print)

Address   Apt. #

City   State/Province   Zip/Postal Code

Email: Please check this box ☐ if you would like to receive newsletters and promotional emails from Harlequin Enterprises ULC and its affiliates. You can unsubscribe anytime.

Mail to the Harlequin Reader Service:
IN U.S.A.: P.O. Box 1341, Buffalo, NY 14240-8531
IN CANADA: P.O. Box 603, Fort Erie, Ontario L2A 5X3

Want to explore our other series or interested in ebooks? Visit www.ReaderService.com or call 1-800-873-8635.

---

*Terms and prices subject to change without notice. Prices do not include sales taxes, which will be charged (if applicable) based on your state or country of residence. Canadian residents will be charged applicable taxes. Offer not valid in Quebec. This offer is limited to one order per household. Books received may not be as shown. Not valid for current subscribers to the Love Inspired or Love Inspired Suspense series. All orders subject to approval. Credit or debit balances in a customer's account(s) may be offset by any other outstanding balance owed by or to the customer. Please allow 4 to 6 weeks for delivery. Offer available while quantities last.

Your Privacy—Your information is being collected by Harlequin Enterprises ULC, operating as Harlequin Reader Service. For a complete summary of the information we collect, how we use this information and to whom it is disclosed, please visit our privacy notice located at https://corporate.harlequin.com/privacy-notice. Notice to California Residents -- Under California law, you have specific rights to control and access your data. For more information on these rights and how to exercise them, visit https://corporate.harlequin.com/california-privacy. For additional information for residents of other U.S. states that provide their residents with certain rights with respect to personal data, visit https://corporate.harlequin.com/other-state-residents-privacy-rights/.